MW00778145

William Jackson

William Jackson is a British author of queer horror fiction. His characters inhabit a homonormative world in stark contrast to the heteronormativity of so much horror narrative. His writing looks at oppression, the inherent seductiveness of evil and the corruption, or moral decay, often masked by beauty. He cites his influences as Richard Laymon, Dennis Wheatley and Fred Mustard Stewart.

Jackson is a master at reaching to the heart of the reader's deepest fears - then deftly twisting his pen. His fiction has been described as *Hammer horror for the 21st Century.*

www.williamjackson.uk

By the same author:

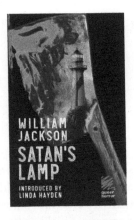

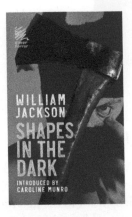

Devil's Rock is the bleakest lighthouse station off the Cornish coast. A lonely rock that locals say is haunted. That's why they call it 'Satan's Lamp'.

Young Jabe Walker, a rookie keeper, is plagued by nightmares of his abusive father - the father Jabe killed when he was just ten years old.

Now it is the 15th of October 1987 and one of the most violent storms in history is about to strike the English coast. On this night Jabe is forced to confront his violent past.

'The writing is hauntingly gentle and spine-chilling in equal measure.'

So writes Caroline Munro in her introduction to this nerve-shredding collection by William Jackson, the new master of gay horror who strikes at the heart of the reader's deepest fears, then twists his pen.

With their deserted lanes and isolated cottages, wolfish men and vampire vixens, his wicked tales have been described as 'Hammer horror for the 21st Century'.

WILLIAM JACKSON

THE SUGAR PIT

INTRODUCED BY
BRITT EKLAND

martin firrell company

First published in 2024 by Martin Firrell Company Ltd. Unit 4 City Limits, Danehill, Reading RG6 4UP, UK.

ISBN 978-1-912622-49-8

Copyright © William Jackson 2024.

William Jackson has asserted his right under the Copyright, Designs and Patents Act 1988 to be identified as the author of this work. This book is a work of fiction. With the exception of historical figures, all names and characters are products of the author's imagination, and any resemblance to actual persons, living or dead, is entirely coincidental. All rights reserved. No part of this publication may be reproduced, stored in or introduced into a retrieval system, or transmitted, in any form, or by any means (electronic, mechanical, photocopying, recording or otherwise) without the prior written consent of the publisher.

This book is sold subject to the condition that it shall not, by way of trade or otherwise, be lent, re-sold, hired out, or otherwise circulated without the publisher's prior consent in any form of binding or cover other than that in which it is published and without a similar condition including this condition being imposed on the subsequent purchaser.

Text is set in Caslon 11pt on 13pt.

for linda hayden

thanks

I would like to thank the following people for the help they gave me as I was writing *The Sugar Pit*. Monna Matharu, Archives Assistant at Library, Archives and Learning Services, University of East London for her help in ascertaining the courses offered by North East London Polytechnic in the late 1980s. Also my publisher Martin Firrell and the team at MFCo: Nathalie Crass-Fielding, Ben Hunter, Grace Onyango-Bell and Paloma Sarsgaard. I would like to thank Danielle Lloyd Edwards, MBACP, for her helpful insights into obsessive behaviours. And thank you to Britt Ekland for her thoughtful and generous introduction to this volume.

introduction by britt ekland

The Sugar Pit is a wicked tale in every sense of that word. And 'wickedness' has played a large part in my acting career in masterpieces of horror like *Endless Night*, *The Wicker Man* and *The Monster Club*, a comedy horror and the last film produced by horror legend Milton Subotsky.

The 'wicked' lets us explore the supernatural, of course, but it also allows us to experience the psychology of power and of power play. Who is dominant? Who is submissive? How do power dynamics work? How do they change?

These are the subjects of William Jackson's superb novel *The Sugar Pit*. We experience both power and powerlessness; both physical power (brute force) and sexual power. The plot of the novel is driven by the very great power of wanting, most especially of wanting what is forbidden.

The Sugar Pit is set in England in the late 1980s when anti-gay laws and discrimination were rife. Jack Huntley

9

is the archetypal product of his time. He looks and sounds and smells like great husband material! His life is gently, reassuringly suburban - it is 'normal' as one might have said back in those days. That's on the surface. Underneath, Jack is a closeted gay man, immensely sexually repressed, and living a lie of a marriage.

He works hard to make things appear a certain way in order to maintain the illusion of normal-ness. He wants to benefit from the advantages that conforming bring him. He wants to be 'the regular guy' when he is anything but. In his defence, the 1980s in the UK were a terrible time to be gay. Jack is not a bad man, just a flawed one.

Even though the story was set in springtime, shooting on the horror classic *The Wicker Man* began in the autumn of 1972. Fake blossoms and leaves had to be stuck onto the trees to create the illusion of spring. I played the pub landlord's daughter Willow. Edward Woodward, Ingrid Pitt and Christopher Lee were my co-stars. When we began shooting against the backdrop of that fake spring, I also found out I was pregnant so some of my nude scenes had to be shot with a body double, for obvious reasons. Nothing is ever as it seems in movies, of course, but this was especially true of *The Wicker Man*.

Nothing is at it seems in *The Sugar Pit*. The hero-husband pretends to desire his wife but what he really desires with a terrible ferocity is the strangely beautiful and mercurial Billy. Billy is the 'sugar' of the title. Billy is the sugar Jack wants to taste and possess. The story is about the needs of the individual (to fit in and to thrive) set against the requirements of society (to oppress any deviance from shared norms).

Policeman Neil Howie (played by Edward Woodward in *The Wicker Man*) soon realises he is living among pagan villagers. The remoteness of their community has allowed them to adopt particularly unusual and terrifying shared norms. Their beliefs are wildly different from, and at odds with, Howie's own.

The people surrounding Jack in *The Sugar Pit* are similarly united in their attitudes, in this instance in their rejection of homosexuality. Jack's obsessive attachment to Billy - to the sweet sugar of possessing Billy - must eventually cast him into a 'pit' of revelation, recrimination and destruction.

Only in his obsessive passion for Billy is Jack truly alive. Only with Billy is Jack honest about who he is. While his wife is away, Jack tastes and touches and holds Billy, living, however briefly, a frankly expressed gay life.

Billy is an exotic pale beauty of a boy, almost Scandinavian in appearance, you might say. But his beauty obscures a much darker nature and an even darker and more desperate heart. Like my character Willow in *The Wicker Man*, Billy will lure a man to his doom. What is beautiful on the outside may be ugly on the inside. Beauty might mask brutality. These are recurring and powerful themes in William Jackson's masterfully constructed novels.

I once played a secretary to a fabulously rich American girl; I was 'Greta' to Hayley Mills' 'Ellie'. The movie was *Endless Night*, directed by Sidney Gilliat and filmed in beautiful locations on the Isle of Wight. Greta plots with Ellie's husband Michael (Hywel Bennet) to murder Ellie for her money. I poison Ellie with bee's venom which gives

11

the impression she has had a heart attack. But when Greta and Michael are discovered and exposed, Michael goes mad with fury, drowning Greta in the swimming pool!

How easily straightforward passion can turn into unhealthy obsession and violence even! Billy becomes an object of wild obsession for Jack and their relationship (a dangerous game of cat-and-mouse like Greta and Michael's) inevitably turns violent.

Billy's chances of getting on in life are limited by society's rejection of his kind. Billy's 'outness' is why he lives in poverty. He won't - or can't - play the game society expects of him. There is a clear-cut material price to be paid.

Jack, on the other hand, has social standing, money and material wealth because he remains hidden. He is not happy, though. His marriage is miserable because it is founded on a deception. The price Jack pays is existential rather than financial.

Mrs X realises Miss Y is her husband's mistress in Strindberg's play, *The Stronger*. Mrs X (played by me in the ITV adaptation) confronts Miss Y (Marianne Faithfull). The two women can be seen as archetypes - opposing aspects of the same man's life.

Similarly, Billy and Jack are alter egos in a world of deception and unfaithfulness. Billy is the alter ego of Jack, the person Jack might have been if he had been stronger. Jack's denial of Billy is a denial of himself, and of his own true nature.

Billy tries to persuade Jack to leave his home, his wife, his child, the whole stifling suburban set-up. Billy wants

Jack to escape to another world - Billy's world. When Jack can't take that step, their relationship turns darker.

It's a simplification, no doubt, but William Jackson's *The Sugar Pit* can be summed up as a gay *Fatal Attraction*. The writing has a vivid and intense cinematic quality. Love and hate are woven tightly together; one cannot exist without the other. It is the story of a casual encounter between two people that turns into something obsessive, then dark, then brutal. With each turn of the page, the heat is turned up and the stakes get higher.

If the hope of giving
is to love the living,
the giver risks madness
in the act of giving.

JAMES BALDWIN

The boy's slender body is pale
as Carrara marble.

chapter one

'NO GAYS'
A cafe on the M25 motorway, which circles London, has put a sign on its door saying, 'No Gays', reports a Gay Times reader.
GAY TIMES, MARCH 1988

i

The curtains are closed against the heat. The bedroom is dark. The boy follows the man into the bedroom and the man and the boy begin to undress. Slowly they reveal themselves to each other. The man is stocky, not quite athletic. The dark hair on his chest funnels neatly down over the faintest impression of abdominal muscle. His face is manly, a little weather-beaten; soft lines arc well formed around his eyes and along his forehead. His face is lightly freckled, his light brown hair is cut in an unfussy short back and sides. He was regarded as 'cute' when he was younger. Nowadays, the women in his circle regard him as the definition of 'husband material'.

He stands naked, priapic now before the boy. Prepotent, a force held in check, he watches the show. And the boy gives him exactly the show he wants. The younger man takes his time undressing: slides off his belt and drops it to the floor, undoes his fly, button by button, steps out of his jeans, slides his satiny briefs down slowly over his thighs and leaves them crumpled at his ankles.

The boy's slender body is pale as Carrara marble. His pubic hair is soft and blond. He is very blond. He is the blondest boy the man has ever seen. He looks at the man with peculiar eyes. It is as if he is looking into the world from somewhere unimaginable.

The man runs his fingers over the boy's smooth chest, touches his blushing nipples and the shallow cleft between his pectoral muscles. He traces a line down to the boy's navel. The boy's skin is cool to the touch. Now the man's answering heat is too impatient to wait any longer. His hunger is undeniable, predatory even. The boy pulls him down onto the bed, opening himself up to him, warm and supple, and the man greases him, and glides in. The man's hips move slowly at first. And then his movements are more urgent, and then each is more remorseless than the last, and his great pent-up heat gushes inside this blondest of all boys and he can't keep himself from crying out the boy's name: 'Billy!'

They lie together, breathing softly in the dark. The boy's white-blond hair is uncannily light. He is a beautiful oddity, an improbability.

18

He looks into the man's soft green eyes: 'You're a great fuck, Jack.'

ii

Four days earlier: Sunday 24th July 1988.

'And Jack, *please* don't forget to put the bin out tomorrow,' my wife said as I brought her cases down from the bedroom.

'You've already mentioned it twice,' I said peevishly. 'I promise I won't forget.'

As usual Lizzie and Thomas were going on ahead to visit my son's grandparents. I would join them later. I suspect Lizzie knew I was glad to be getting some time to myself: quiet time in the house, pottering in the garden. A few summer days free of distractions or interruptions. Bliss.

Lizzie and I had taken out a large mortgage to buy *Claia Bourne*. The house was bigger than we needed really: four bedrooms, and a good-sized garden backing onto the golf course. It was built in the 1930s when Westward Hatch was still a small village, a little before London's inexorable expansion into the landscape after the Second World War. On top of hefty repayments there were the car loans, council rates and Thomas's school fees. 'Keeping up with the Joneses' was expensive and stressful.

'There's leftover lasagne in the fridge.' Lizzie fiddled anxiously with a strand of auburn hair. She was poring over her 'to do' list. She didn't like driving and I knew she wasn't looking forward to the long journey north. 'And take it easy on the Indian takeaways. They make the house smell.' She fluttered around like a deranged bird, dropping a holdall of Thomas's toys by the front door, checking the money in her purse, reminding, re-emphasising, double-checking: 'The window cleaner's due on Thursday. His money's next to the bread bin. Go to the bank and pay the gas bill. Put up those shelves in Thomas's room if you can. Nora's not coming this week so don't make a mess.' (People say the tenth year of marriage is the hardest.) Our housekeeper, Nora, was a jovial force of nature from Donegal and I was going to miss her help around the house. I helped Lizzie load up her car then hugged my seven-year-old son.

'Be a good boy for nanny and grandad,' I said. He smiled. His brown eyes were bright and eager under the floppy curls he'd inherited from his mother. I made a mental note to get his hair cut. 'Daddy will be up at the end of the week.'

'Thursday afternoon!' Lizzie said in an emphatic tone, slamming the boot shut.

'Should be. If I get everything sorted at school. Friday latest.' I tousled Thomas's hair as I strapped him into the passenger seat. I kissed Lizzie, holding her close, feeling the warmth of her body.

Like touching through glass.

Lizzie's silver Fiesta disappeared down The Avenue with Thomas waving enthusiastically to the last. I turned back towards the house. Its facade was a perfect imitation of Tudor. Not the real thing. The candlestick chimneys had been saved from the ruins of Lambourne Hall. Now they kept an uneasy watch over suburbia, over the tree-lined Avenue, over neat front gardens and the pristine turf of the golf course.

The garden shed smelled of sun-baked wood and petrol. Lizzie never came in here. I kept my cache in a cardboard box beside the lawnmower. I brushed the cobwebs off. The first few magazines were old copies of *Practical Gardening* monthly, then came the copies of *Mister*, then *Vulcan*, then one solitary copy of *Zipper*. I had bought it out of curiosity but soon realised muscle men weren't really my thing. I picked out a *Mister*, an old favourite and went back into the house, up to the guest room, and lay on the bed.

iii

The sheets are cool against my nakedness. It's a while since I've had a moment to myself like this. My wife and son are always here. I am lightheaded as I turn the pages. I am very aware of my hands, of the fine dark hairs in the skin. I like my hands. The moment begins to stretch out like a bead of water sliding down a misted window.

I contemplate the parade of young men. They are temptation frozen in time. They are mine. A young man, naked from the waist down, stares moodily at the camera as he plays with the collar of his oversized dress shirt.

Tony, a bleached blond with studded collar and leather boots, crouches on all fours.

The young guy in the centrefold is completely naked but for two gold loop earrings and a Chinese charm necklace. He is down on one knee, smooth-skinned apart

21

from a little downy boyish hair spread over his calves and shins. He is circumcised. He has an air of tough vulnerability. He is mine, too.

This young male beauty is definitely mine.

I choose him for my fantasy. I imagine him in my arms. I imagine tasting his lips. I imagine taking him deep. I spread my legs and close my right hand around my shaft and ride my tough and vulnerable boy. My passion releases rapidly and I clean myself up and drift away into sleep.

iv

The centrefold was still propped open on the pillow beside me. It was my eloquent accuser now. I was a pansy, a bender, a bum-boy, an arse-bandit, a poofter, a queer. There were so many god-awful names for it. Naked-but-for-gold-loop-earrings-and-a-Chinese-charm-necklace was proof enough of my 'inversion'.

Lizzie I cared for, but didn't really desire. My son I adored. But beyond that lay a shadowland of pubs and clubs and boys. There was a masochistic sweetness to all this; there was always the danger of being discovered; there was always the danger of AIDS, all set against my restless, undeniable compulsion for sex with men.

I mowed the lawn, cut back the laurels, went for a walk around the golf course, ate reheated lasagne, read Bret Easton Ellis's *The Rules of Attraction*, shut the curtains against the night, slept.

The traffic was lighter than usual. It was the first day of the summer holidays. 'Enjoy the holidays, Mr Huntley.' 'Have a nice rest, sir!' 'See you in September!' The kids always assumed it was six weeks of indolence for us as well. A long list of jobs waited for me. As deputy head, I had to review subject co-ordinators' yearly plans. I had to complete a school-wide stock take. I had to draw up next year's timetables. I had to find time, somehow, to tidy and decorate my own classroom. Old displays had to be taken down and fresh backing paper stapled to walls. I had to review handover notes on my next class. I had to clear out the store cupboard. Had to. Had to. Had to. All the time.

(*Mister magazine for handsome models, the guy next door.*)

Over a third of our kids were from Turkish or Greek backgrounds (Roughton Road Primary sat between Bush Hill Park and Chase Side). Car stickers declared their fathers' loyalty to Galatasaray or Olympiacos.

I always got the toughest class in Year Six. The most recent cohort were tougher than usual. Even after all these years, the casual cruelty of children could take my breath away.

The girls formed spiteful little friendship groups. Anyone who broke the rules of the clique was mercilessly victimised until I'd find them sobbing in my classroom, afraid to go out into the yard at break time.

The boys extorted money for girlie magazines stolen from the local newsagent. Or invented ugly playground games, often dividing along racial or religious lines: 'Greeks versus Turks', 'Christians versus Muslims'. Things got out of hand one day when Mehmet Yilmaz (overweight, Turkish, nice lad) was smeared with faeces in the boys' toilets.

My class's parting shot was scrawled across the blackboard: 'Mr Huntley's gay'. You couldn't say fairer than that. But true or not, the ragged scrawl had to go. I was rubbing it out when the boss, Sandie, popped her head around the door.

Sandie got on well with Lizzie; and her husband, Nigel, was my doubles partner at the tennis club. They often invited us over for dinner. He would ply me with drink, invariably finishing with 'one more for the road?' Lizzie was careful to limit herself to two glasses of white wine. Sandie had no trouble working her way through a whole bottle. Sandie and Nigel were a little older than us with kids at university. I imagined Sandie drank to fill the emptiness of the empty nest. When we returned the invitation to dinner, Lizzie's preparations resembled a military exercise. I ribbed her repeatedly about 'keeping up with the Batesons'. Most recently, she'd served up a salad with grilled halloumi, salmon wellington and a perfect, homemade tart tatin.

(*Vulcan for sweet, beautiful, waif-like boys.*)

It was my job to organise the wine, cheese and nibbles and keep Thomas out from under mummy's feet. I usually took him to MacDonald's after dragging him around Fortnum and Mason's.

24

'Jack! Just the person!' Sandie said. 'Have you got a minute? My office. And good morning by the way.'

I made coffee and opened a packet of digestives. Sandy moved folders and stacks of papers from her desk. *(Tony is naked from the waist down – his legs are hairless and smooth.)* We discussed the latest directives from Enfield LEA on the Education Reform Act and the new National Curriculum. Sandie sounded me out on the possibility of Roughton Road becoming grant-maintained, something our fiercely left-leaning staff would oppose *(in studded collar and leather boots)*.

'How are the new timetables coming, Jack?'

'Year Three and Four are done. I'll have the rest finished by Wednesday*(crouching on all fours)*.'

'Marvellous. Any problems?'

'Just the usual. No one wants to do P.E. last lesson, and no one wants to do the first class assembly in September.'

'That's why you always do it, Mr Huntley.' Sandie nudged me encouragingly.

'I'm all heart.'*(Completely naked, down on all fours.)*

'And how's that gorgeous little boy of yours?'

'He's fine. Growing up too fast. Lizzie's taken him to see her parents in the Peaks. I'm going later on this week.'

'I hope she's left you enough supplies. I know what you boys are like - burger and chips and a couple of pints every night.'

'All supplies are packaged up and labelled. You know Lizzie.'

'Before I forget, Nigel wants to know if you're still on for the doubles match tomorrow?'

'Definitely.'

(Tony is uncircumcised.)

'And I've swapped things round a little for September. The probationer's going to be in the classroom opposite yours. And you'll be mentoring him.'

(Vulcan magazine for sweet, beautiful, waif-like boys.)

Andy Church was a fresh-faced lad straight out of teacher training college and one of the last probationers left on the local authority teaching pool. The high-flyers were snapped up quickly by the best schools whereas Roughton Road was a difficult environment with a bad reputation.

Andy's mentor was supposed to be Muriel Parker-Ross but I understood Sandie's change of heart. Muriel was often off ill with difficult-to-pin-down ailments. She was just back from maternity leave.

She also had to contend with Ricky Bridgewood in her class, starved of oxygen at birth, an SEN boy. He was never going to progress beyond a mental age of four. Ricky didn't cope very well with change, so it had been decided that Muriel would stay with his class and take him up into Year Four. Sandie and I had been applying to get some permanent classroom support but the LEA as usual was dragging its feet, blaming funding cuts.

Our own budget was incredibly tight, but we did what we could. Classes were allocated a pitiful amount of stationery per term. Inevitably children mislaid (or stole) things, so we were all buying extra packs of pencils, rulers, rubbers and crayons with our own money.

Most school equipment was old and unreliable and

tempers often frayed. Sandie and I were often on the receiving end of our colleagues' frustrations.

(*Mister magazine for handsome models, the guy next door.*)

Andy Church would need support in his probationary year, especially at a school like Roughton Road. Andy could turn into yet another headache. But I liked his youth and leanness and his mass of black hair. His face was serious and softly handsome in a way that reminded me of Sargent's portrait of Edward Vickers (Poor Edward, painted at twenty-one, dead at twenty-four). We loaded a trolley with brightly-coloured exercise books: blue for English, orange for maths, green for topic work. We also took several rolls of backing paper and a staple gun from the stock room.

Back in my own classroom, I made a start, ripping down the old displays and bundling them into black bin bags. When I checked in on Andy half an hour later, he was making a dog's breakfast of smoothing backing paper against his classroom wall. I suggested the pub for lunch.

The Painter's Arms was a five-minute drive away on the other side of the Great Cambridge Road. Monday lunchtimes were invariably quiet and we settled into a corner by the window. Andy sat hunched like an accused man waiting for the judge. I probably made him nervous. He seemed too much of a kid himself to be taking charge of a class of thirty. He bulldozed his tuna baguette like it was the first proper meal he'd had in days. Maybe it was.

'What made you decide on teaching?' I asked.

'History degree,' he mumbled cautiously. 'Teaching seemed like the only option. Plus my mum was a teacher before she gave up work to have kids.'

'Are you still living at home?'

'No, I've got a flat-share with a couple of girls from teacher training. They're both going to teach secondary at the same school in Tottenham.'

'Are you looking forward to starting in September?'

'I want to enjoy the summer break first. The course was pretty full-on.'

'PGCEs always are.'

'How long have you been teaching?'

'Twelve years.'

'The job must have changed a fair bit since you started.'

'Especially with Thatcher. There'll be more and more scrutiny.'

(Tony is naked from the waist down.)

'Won't that be a good thing?'

'Not if it turns into a witch hunt - hunting down subversive lefties in jeans and tee shirts telling the kids to call them by their first names. I've never met anybody like that in my twelve years. There'll be more paperwork, more accounting for every little thing. More stress.' The boy looked a little panicked. Jesus, Jack! Come on, I thought to myself, you're the deputy head for Christ's sake! I caressed the neck of my bottle of Molson *(his chest is firm, his nipples thick)*. 'Teaching's always been tough but, as they say, it's a vocation, not a job. And there's never a dull moment at Roughton Road.'

'You mean I've got some characters in my class?' His smile lit up saddle-brown eyes. Andy had a nice smile.

'Oh yes. There's no shortage of those.'

28

I spent most of the afternoon helping Andy get his classroom straight. When I got home I watched the Test Match from Headingley, the fourth day of England versus the West Indies. It wasn't looking good for our boys.

Lizzie picked up on the third ring. Her parents sent their love. She'd taken Thomas shopping in Manchester; the Arndale was packed but she'd got herself a new cocktail dress and Thomas a pair of trainers. When she put Thomas on the phone, he was brimful of how he'd beaten grandad three times at Hungry Hippos. Part of me felt glad and part of me aggrieved, forgotten.

I thought about Andy. It felt good thinking about Andy. I retrieved my magazine and stretched out on the bed.

The air in the room was still, arrested in that interval between the heat of the day and cool of the night.

vi

I am thinking about Andy. I flip-flop through the magazine. Here's Tony. His hair is thick like Andy's but it's in a rockabilly style. He is slim like Andy and he comes across as shy, like Andy. The boy is naked, uncircumcised. And it makes me wonder is Andy cut or uncut? *The boy is on all fours.* I reach down into my briefs, stroking myself as I imagine him standing in front of me. I imagine taking hold of him, roughly kissing his neck, his lips, pushing him to his knees; I imagine the boy looking up at me.

Ready.

But he isn't real.

This time, he isn't enough.

I lie back against the pillow. And, there it is, the sweet ache between my legs. Like a form of hunger.

I am a wayward boy again, driven by my burgeoning desire, remembering a July afternoon in 1968; the back of the cricket pavilion; Digby Willoughby; cricket whites; dark wood warm against our backs; a light breeze rolling across the playing field; Digby slim and tanned; Digby's indefinable beauty not quite male not quite female; arctic blue eyes; Digby's hand touching mine; Digby's hand against mine again; my hand against his knee; our lips together; that unearthly moment; tentative and tender; soft kisses; then my tongue inside his mouth; our tongues dancing; the world becoming more distant as we kiss; as we masturbate; Digby's breath faster and heavier; our coming together in the moment.

And then the guilt; later my mother's condemnations of homosexuals, portrayed on the telly, as 'sick and wrong'; and then my real shame: my silence; as the other boys called him 'poofter', 'shirt-lifter'; my silence as they blow him kisses; call him 'nice boy' in affected voices, punch him in the gut; my silence as they trash his school books; stick his head down the toilet; *Come and see the blue goldfish, Willoughby, Willy-boy, Willy-sucker;* my silence as he suffers it all; Jesus on the Via Dolorosa. And as I, Peter to his Christ, deny him, deny him, deny him.

I go into the bathroom and brush my teeth. It will take about an hour to get into town. I get dressed, slip off my wedding ring and put it on the bedside table.

As I start out towards the station, the sycamores are casting weak shadows on The Avenue in the last of the summer light.

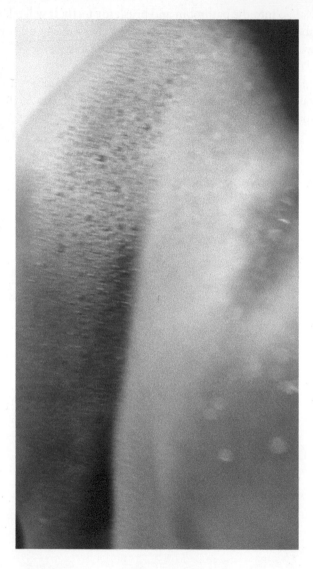

Jack feels the heat of Billy's slim young body and his skin smells fresh and soapy and it's as if he's only just washed.

chapter two

i

Superfly Guy thundering through the smoke-blue air; poppers, banana-sweet; men in a predatory swarm in the tightly-packed space; everyone shouting to be heard; the mass of maleness at the bar; hard, sculpted bodies, figure-hugging vests, lumberjack shirts; laughing and drinking and teasing each other; and it's difficult to imagine any of them growing old; and many of them won't.

Jack spots a narrow gap in the line at the bar and sidles in. He leans across the counter in an effort to catch the barman's eye. The name of the bar and an upturned pink triangle decorate the barman's snug white tee. Barman cranes his shaven head in Jack's direction and Jack orders a pint of Stella. He scans the room: men with goatees and peaked leather caps; men as clones sporting buzz cuts and neatly trimmed moustaches; boys - not quite men - with 501s and slicked-back hair; Nick Kamen wannabes.

Now Jack's gaze finds the one oddity in the place; white-blond hair; black leather trousers; a studded belt slung low across slim hips; a gold stud in each ear; dancing by himself at the centre of the room.

At Jack's smile he grins in return and Jack beckons him over. 'Is this your usual haunt?' Jack begins.

'Not really. Me and my mates like to flit around a bit.'

'Where are your mates tonight?'

'Dunno. Busy. Is this your local, then?'

'No it's not. How old are you?'

'Twenty. How old are you?'

'Thirty-six. Way too old for you.'

'That's for me to decide.'

Now the oddity is shoved suddenly into Jack's arms by the boisterous crowd and Jack feels the heat of his slim young body; and his skin smells fresh and soapy and it's as if he's only just washed; and Jack manoeuvres him away from the dancers, makes a shield of himself to protect the boy from the jostling crowd.

'Thank you,' the boy says, and his hands are resting gently on Jack's forearms. 'Billy!'

'Jack!'

Billy's smile emphasises his youth. But there's something bleak behind it all, evident briefly, before it dissolves into cheerfulness again.

'What do you do?' Billy asks.

'I'm a teacher.'

'I'm a student. D'you go to the gay teachers group?'

'Never heard of it.'

Billy says he's studying at NELP, reading Applied Linguistics. He didn't fancy college at first, but then twelve

34

months lackeying in a betting shop changed his mind. He is taking refuge in education while he works out what to do with his life, and he's trying to make himself heard over the Eurobeat shaking the room; and his breath is in Jack's ear and it's sending a sweet tingling down Jack's neck; and now Jack slips an arm around the boy's narrow waist and the boy reciprocates; and Jack kisses him roughly on the mouth and Billy puts his arms around Jack's shoulders, melting into him as Jack squeezes him tight, pulling him closer still.

Jack hasn't held or kissed another man for months. A while back, he'd managed to steal an hour at the Coleherne on Old Brompton Road. Large, crowded, anonymous, a notorious meat market - perfect. The man was the same age as Jack. He invited Jack to a sorry bedsit. Clones weren't really Jack's type but he needed sex. He needed the feel of another man's body warm against his own. He was careful not to get a rash from the guy's greying stubble. He made sure they were safe. He always made sure.

Afterwards he felt the usual low.

Billy is slim and young and impulsive with an off-kilter charm, and Jack takes him outside; and the street lamps on St. Martin's Lane are already lit against the quickening dusk. The pubs and restaurants lend the street splashes of warm golden light and Jack and Billy catch a cab to Billy's.

Billy tells Jack he got the flat through the East of London Housing Association; he shares it with another gay student but he's away so they'll have the place to themselves. Jack follows him up a narrow concrete staircase; the banister is painted with thick black paint and the hall is starkly lit. The front door is heavy, burglar proof. Billy turns his key in the lock and Jack notices the strip of dimly patterned carpet in the hallway.

Jack sits at Billy's kitchen table; the surface is scarred with rings from hot coffee mugs, and he watches Billy pull two cups from a pile of dirty crockery and turn to fill the electric kettle; and the black leather is taught across Billy's buttocks and Jack can see the line of his briefs underneath; and he gets up and takes hold of the boy, licking the nape of his neck like a dog and says, 'Why don't we forget the coffee?'

Jack kisses him for a long time. The bedroom is a tiny box with a single bed shoved into the corner opposite a tatty wardrobe. Posters of Harrison Ford, Bruce Willis and Richard Gere. A naked electric bulb hanging from the ceiling. Jack throws the boy onto the bed and pulls off his own shirt and jeans; and the boy lies on his back, gazing up at Jack almost lovingly and Jack watches him strip and Billy slides open the drawer of his bedside table, and fishes out a packet of Mates and a bottle of poppers.

Billy unscrews the lid and breathes in deep, then holds the bottle under Jack's nose; and Jack climbs onto him, and feels a familiar panicky rush; and the blood is pounding in his head now; and his heart is at full gallop, thudding and thundering wildly; and his craving for Billy's nakedness is savage - simply that; and he runs his hands forcefully over Billy's soft skin, and the boy's ankles are resting on his shoulders, and then he is inside him and taking him and fucking him and fucking and fucking and fucking him.

When Jack wakes up it's light outside. Billy is gone and Jack's neck is stiff from lying awkwardly on the narrow bed. The sound of Capital Breakfast drifts down the hallway. Jack finds Billy in the kitchen and leans over him, smelling his milk-white skin, and their lips touch.

'Morning, green eyes,' Billy says, touching Jack's face with long white fingers.

'That was quite a night.' Jack wants to bed him again already, fuck him all day, shut the world out. But he has to go to work. He takes the coffee and toast Billy offers and sits down at the table.

'How long have you been married?'

So that's a sucker punch from nowhere. Billy takes Jack's hand and turns it over in his own, and says matter-of-factly, 'Your wedding ring has left a tan line.'

'Nearly ten years.'

'What's her name?'

'Lizzie.'

'Nice name,' Billy says. 'Do you love her?'

'I don't know. I did once. Time fades things I guess.'

'Do you regret it, getting married?'

'It seemed like the right thing to do at the time.'

'To avoid suspicion?'

'No, not because of that. I've been fighting against being like this. It's hard. I'm not as relaxed with it all as you are.'

'How do you know I don't have a wife of my own?' Billy giggles. The idea is absurd. When Billy Soanes left the closet, he left the door swinging on broken hinges.

37

'Haven't you ever thought of starting fresh, being honest with everyone?' But Jack doesn't want to hear it. Not now, not here, with Billy.

'I guess it's too late for that,' he says. 'I've made my bed. I've got a job, a reputation.'

'All that crap?'

'Yes. All that crap. And I have a little boy. I have to think of him.' And with that, Jack shuts Billy down.

'Forget I said anything,' Billy says, touching Jack's cheek. 'This is just a bit of fun.'

Jack stuffs Billy's phone number in his back pocket as he leaves. Billy stands at the open door, and looks at him hazily, and he reminds Jack of something: a child saying goodbye to a parent.

ii

My clothes reeked of tobacco and sweat. I went home to change and made it into school just after half past ten.

'You're looking rather raffish this morning, Mr Huntley,' Sandie said, looking at me steadily. 'Are you growing a beard?'

'I overslept. Didn't have time to shave.'

'Lizzie's only been away a couple of days.' She raised her eyebrows. 'Don't worry, I won't squeal on you.'

Like all teachers I was a professional hoarder, holding on to anything and everything in the hope it might be useful one day. Now was the time to bite the bullet and clear out the store cupboard. I junked old text books, dried up bottles of poster paint, broken protractors and compasses, and word games I'd never used.

Andy came by and asked if I could go through the reading scheme with him. He seemed more at ease with me this time. By quarter to three I could feel a vague muzziness in my head; last night's passion and the day's stifling heat catching up with me. Andy was familiar enough with the reading scheme so I decided to call it a day. Sandie caught me as I was leaving. 'Are you going to the club early?'

'Damn!' I said. 'I totally forgot. I've left my racquet at home. I'll miss the rush hour if I go now and be back by four. Can you let Nigel know I might be a few minutes late?'

'Sure,' she said slowly. 'It's not like you to forget your beloved tennis.'

I splashed cold water on my face, changed into my tennis whites and hurried out to join Nigel on court three. It was our second fixture in the annual summer tournament. We'd just scraped through on a tie-break in our opening match and now we were up against Rod Gregson and Pete Norland. They were two of the best doubles players at the club. Both were several inches taller than us, which gave them a dangerous advantage. We won the toss and decided to serve first.

I opened the match by serving two double faults in a row. Most of my backhands glided well past the baseline and my overhead smashes slammed straight into the net. I was angry with myself and that led inevitably to more needless mistakes.

'It just wasn't our moment,' Nigel said, giving me a consoling slap on the belly as we washed off our defeat in the showers.

'I don't know what's wrong with me,' I said.

But I did know. My mind wasn't on the game. My mind was on Billy. *Billy*. I didn't want to play tennis with Nigel, I wanted to go to bed with Billy. Billy was the best sex I'd had in a very long time and I wanted more. I dug out Billy's number and called him from a payphone and he picked up almost instantly.

I said no to Nigel's offer of a pint and drove home via the Chinese. I left lemon chicken warming in the oven and went to collect Billy from the station.

iii

Billy stands in the front hall, hands thrust in the pockets of his jeans, wriggling like an over-excited schoolboy. Evening light streams in through the windows, throwing criss-cross patterns, like a fishing net, over his young face.

'Nice place,' he grins.

Jack breaks open a couple of beers and they spread the takeaway cartons over the table in the sitting room. Billy eats quickly and talks fast, describing people from college (people Jack knows he's never going to meet). Billy shines a merciless light on their quirks and failings. Everybody is fair game: tutors, students, counsellors, librarians. He is an exceptional mimic, and his impressions give Jack a good idea of each of Billy's victims.

Billy tells Jack he had an affair with his high school form tutor; he is an only child; his father died young; his mother is schizophrenic and an alcoholic.

40

Something flickers behind Billy's starry-eyed youthfulness and something corresponds in Jack, and Jack would like to take Billy away from his cramped flat share, from seedy bars and clubs, and give him something better.

But that is not in his gift.

He moves closer to the boy until their bodies meet; presses his tongue between the boy's lips, inside his mouth now, softly tugging on the boy's lower lip as he withdraws. He covers the boy with his body, closing his hands over his, feeling him, young and slight underneath him.

The phone rings.

'Don't move,' he says. 'I'll be right back.'

'Jack?' Lizzie sounds concerned. 'Where have you been? I phoned earlier.'

'Nigel and I had that match, remember? We went for a pint then I stopped off to pick up a Chinese.'

'What about that casserole I left in the freezer?'

'Forgot to get it out.'

'Get it out now. You can have it tomorrow.'

'How's things?' Suddenly Billy's hands are on his waist. He grunts.

'Are you okay?' Lizzie asks.

'Sure. I'm just a bit achy after the game.'

'How did it go?'

'We lost.'

Billy kisses his neck, tickling with the tip of his tongue, and his breath is hot on the skin, and Jack squirms out of his grasp and almost drops the phone.

'It's been pouring here all day,' says Lizzie. 'We took Thomas to the science museum.'

'I bet he loved it.'

'He didn't want to leave. What time can we expect you on Thursday?'

'I'll set off mid-morning, so late afternoon.'

'Your son wants to speak to you.'

Thomas talks excitedly about hot air engines and locomotives, and Jack signals to Billy to get more beers from the fridge.

Then Lizzie is back on the phone.

'Thomas is full of beans,' Jack says. 'Sounds like he's had a wonderful time.' Billy pinches Jack lightly under the ribs and it takes all his effort not to make a sound.

'Are you okay, darling?' Lizzie says. 'You sound a little strange.'

'I'm fine. Just miffed about losing the game. Nigel was on top form. I wasn't. I let him down.'

'There'll be other tournaments. Nigel doesn't take it as seriously as you. Remember that. How's work?'

'Lots to do still. We've got a new probationer starting in September and Sandie has asked me to mentor him.'

'That'll be no problem, will it?' There's anxiety in Lizzie's voice. Any change in routine is a source of worry to her, the seeds of a potential crisis or disaster.

Jack wants to get her off the phone.

'I'd better go. The takeaway's burning in the oven.'

He finds Billy lying where he left him.

'I haven't moved an inch,' Billy says, winking.

'Liar.'

'You're a pretty good liar yourself.' He mimics Jack on the phone perfectly: 'My takeaway's burning in the oven.'

'A white lie,' Jack says.

Now they are in the guest room and they take their time with each other. The boy unbuttons Jack's shirt and nibbles at his neck, making him flinch.

'Careful! I don't want a bloody love bite.'

'Sorry.' Billy kisses him tenderly on the same spot. 'Don't worry. There's no incriminating evidence here. The fish and chips will be none the wiser.'

'Fish and chips?'

'Wife and kids.'

'I haven't heard that one before.' Jack presses his finger to the boy's lips before he can say any more.

Billy closes his eyes in response to the firm pressure of Jack's hands on his body. Jack strips Billy of his clothes, then takes off his own. Everything happens very slowly. Jack wants to extend the moment for as long as possible. Skin brushes skin. Lips touch lightly. Slow sensation. Slow. Exquisite. Slow. Excruciating sensation.

Then the cold-water thought occurs to Jack: I've never asked anyone back to the house before; the risk is impossibly great. He imagines tidying up, putting things back after Billy has gone; everything, anything, to eradicate Billy, but then Billy kisses him and kisses him again and they are moving slowly against one another, and they are hungry for the contours of each other's bodies, and Jack reaches the point of no return suddenly and surrenders; and Billy laughs; and slowly, theatrically, finishes himself off.

Jack sleeps for a long time. The world returns in the soft light of the portable TV. Billy is watching David Soul spying on a woman as she undresses in her apartment. Jack has spent his whole marriage in much the same way - looking at Lizzie as if from a distance. He has been acting a part, of course. He has been going through the motions. He is afraid to let anyone get close to the real Jack Huntley, if there is a real Jack Huntley. He has always been afraid.

But now, in the half-light, holding Billy in his arms, he feels real to himself. This is real. This is a real life. He doesn't want to go away on Thursday. He wants to stay with Billy, here, at Claia Bourne.

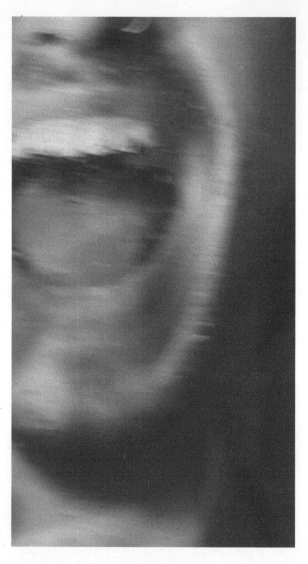

With Billy it was different; I was a driver
on the race track, intent on the win.

chapter three

i

Billy leans in at the car window smiling like a sexy cherub. Jack notices the boy's eyes are two slightly different shades of blue and he wonders why he hadn't seen it before. It's a handsome peculiarity and seductive and strange, like so much about Billy.

Billy.

A young couple are walking arm-in-arm past the car and Jack's hoping Billy isn't expecting to kiss him, not here, not out in public. He sits there, gripping the steering wheel as if his life depended on it.

'See you later,' Billy says.

'Sure, 6pm.'

'You okay? You seem on edge.'

'I've just got a lot to do today.'

'Then I'd better let you get on with it.'

It wasn't just the fear of being spotted in public. I knew I was playing a very dangerous game; I'd been with other men before but I'd never been to bed with any of them more than once; I'd never brought any of them back to the house. With Billy it was different; this was new and electrifying and terrifying; I was a driver on the race track, intent on the win, taking the bends just a little too fast.

I turned the plan over and over in my mind, looking for holes but I couldn't find any.

Just before 3pm, I told Sandie my back was playing up. It was a small lie based on a larger truth. I'd had an accident back in my boy-racer days: I was trying to avoid the rush hour traffic on Lea Bridge Road so I'd driven into the maze of backstreets between Leyton Green and Whipps Cross; I came to a crossroads with cars parked on either side, cars too close to the junction, parked cars everywhere making it impossible to see properly; and I was impatient to get home to watch the Wimbledon semi-finals so I pressed on regardless; and there was a sickening crunch and a Ford Capri smashed into the side of me and I was sent spinning. The car was a write-off and I didn't fare much better myself. I hit my head hard and ended up with a concussion and feeling generally unwell for days afterwards. The doctor signed me off for a week. The other driver walked away without a scratch: he'd been wearing a seatbelt. Then a tingling sensation developed down the left side of my back, made worse whenever I overstretched or lifted something heavy. X-rays showed curvature of the spine.

'I must have thrown my back out during the match

yesterday,' I lied, hoping Sandie would buy it.

She could be a tough customer when it came to sick leave. 'You poor thing,' she said, squeezing my arm. 'Will you be all right getting home?'

'I can manage at the moment but not if it gets any worse.'

'How's our probationer getting on?'

'Andy's pretty much sorted. I've shown him the ropes. Most of them, anyway.'

'What about you, Mr Huntley? Have you got everything done that you needed to?'

'Pretty much. The timetables for next term are on your desk.'

Sandie seemed satisfied. 'Get home and rest up. Will you still be able to visit the in-laws tomorrow?'

'I hope so,' I lied again. 'I'll see how I feel in the morning.' (Lizzie and Thomas weren't coming back until Monday night and I planned to spend the rest of the week and all weekend with Billy.)

I stopped off at Jay Jay's on The Broadway for the usual supplies when left to my own devices: alcohol, crisps, chocolate. I also went into the video shop run by a friendly Italian family and fronted by their eldest son Donnie, a lovely dark-eyed youth. I was a trusted regular and Donnie let me look in 'The Box' whenever the shop was empty.

'The Box' was kept under the counter and contained the latest pirate videos. This year I'd watched *Beetlejuice*, *Dirty Rotten Scoundrels* and *Bull Durham* while they were still on at the cinema. The shop was busy so I had to settle for browsing the shelves with all the other customers. Most of the best films were already taken. I didn't know what

49

Billy would like so I hedged my bets with *Beverly Hills Cop* and *A View to a Kill*.

The sky was an unnatural, garish blue as I turned onto The Avenue.

I took a long lazy shower, slathered myself in cologne and picked out a denim shirt, rolling the sleeves up to my elbows.

I decided to call Lizzie before collecting Billy from the station.

'For Christ's sake, Jack! I can't believe it.'

'I'm really sorry. I felt it go in the game yesterday and it's just got worse since then.'

'Your son will be very disappointed.'

I'd been waiting for that. When Lizzie wanted to bring me into line, Thomas was her weapon of choice. She'd conjure the picture of a wounded child neglected by a distant, unloving father who was always working, always with more important things to do.

'Can't you get an appointment at the osteo?'

'I tried. He's booked up.'

'I'll phone him.'

'Don't do that. I've already pleaded with his secretary,' I lied again.

'We'll come back tomorrow, then.'

'No,' I said, perhaps a little too forcefully. 'You guys stay and have a good time. The last thing I want is to spoil your holiday.'

I wanted to put down the receiver and walk away.

'Thomas misses you. It's hardly surprising as I'm always having to play bad cop to your good cop.'

'That's not fair.'

'I think it is.'

'You're the full-time mum. Of course you have to crack the whip more often than I do. Has he been playing up?'

'No. It's just that he gets spoilt by his grandparents and then I have to rein him in. And my mum's been giving me her usual 'helpful tips' on child-rearing.'

'Just nod and smile, darling.'

'I miss you Jack.'

The words threw an ugly spotlight on what I was about to do.

'I miss you too.'

'You'd better tell your son you're not coming,' was Lizzie's parting shot.

iii

When Jack gets Billy back to the house he pours them both a hefty glass of whisky. He wants this time to be happy and easy. For both their sakes.

In truth, he's a little envious of Billy, of his freedom and his easy acceptance of who he is. Jack would like to know what it's like to live in Billy's world; he'd like to know what it would feel like to open his eyes each day and see another man lying next to him, just like any other ordinary couple. Except not ordinary, not like that at all.

He tells Billy about his year out - when he was Billy's age - backpacking across the Far East: Singapore, Bali, India. He'd travelled with a girl he was seeing at the time, a friend of one of his cousins, a pretty brunette called Lucy.

But they broke up halfway through the trip. It was the

first time she'd been away without her parents. She wasn't used to backpacking and everything that went with it. One night she found a cockroach in the communal bathroom and screamed like she was being murdered. He told her she needed to get used to that sort of thing; there'd be plenty more of it on their way, and then they started arguing. She said he should have taken her travelling in Europe, somewhere a bit more 'upmarket'. After that, their romantic adventure was pretty much done.

Billy's world travels amounted to a day at Alton Towers and a school trip to north Wales. He'd never been abroad; didn't own a passport.

But in other ways Billy is far more adventurous. Billy is 'out and proud' as he calls it. Billy is a brave kid in a world where 'pretty policemen' entrap gay men and a deputy headteacher can lose his job if he comes out.

Jack wants some air - needs some air - so he and Billy go for a walk by the golf course.

The gorse is in flower and the air is sickly sweet with its odd coconut-ish scent; and the rabbits have been busy digging and nibbling at the edges of the green; and Billy takes hold of Jack's wrist and leads him into the rough next to one of the bunkers. Jack glances around him nervously but the greens and fairways are empty. Billy stops suddenly and lies down on his back and the chirping of grasshoppers fills the air and the bright little chirp-chirp, chirp-chirp rhythm is lazy and hot and hypnotic; and 'Fuck me,' Billy whispers. 'Fuck me right here. Right now.' And he pulls down his jeans, and reveals snug red briefs.

'Jesus, Billy!' In spite of himself, Jack feels himself getting hard. 'Get up, for Christ's sake!' He tries to pull up the boy's jeans, pull him to his feet but the boy wriggles free. 'Stop it,' Jack tells him. 'Someone could come at any minute.'

Billy is laughing. 'Yeah, you or me.'

'Don't be so bloody stupid!' Jack starts walking away. 'Some of the neighbours are club members.' The nightmare image flashes across his mind: *One of the neighbours is walking towards him. 'Hey, Jack,' he calls, 'what are you doing over there?' And then he sees Billy lying there on his back.*

Billy comes running after him, buttoning himself up. 'What's the problem? I was just messing about.'

'It's not funny. I know people round here. It's not fucking Hampstead Heath.'

'Okay. I get it!' They walk in silence, and the spell is broken and this isn't how it's supposed to be. Jack loops his little finger around Billy's.

'But I'll fuck your brains out when we get back,' he says.

They order pizza and snuggle up. Billy isn't keen on cop films so they abandon Eddie Murphy and settle down to Roger Moore. But Jack is impatient; he takes Billy to bed before the film is over. The boy is silky and supple; he is warm milk and honey. Jack squeezes the boy tightly.

There once was a boy who was given a kitten and he loved the kitten so much because of its little pink nose and soft downy fur and the way it went 'mew, mew' and he couldn't stop squeezing and squeezing the beloved little cat until one day he squeezed it to death. True story.

Jack wakes at half past three. Billy is lying with his back to him. The night is thick and hot and from then on Jack sleeps fitfully, his mind replaying the call with Lizzie. He isn't the dutiful husband nursing a bad back. He's a dirty liar, fucking a boy he picked up in a sleazy basement bar.

He shifts onto his side and Billy stirs next to him, whimpering and twitching and Jack guesses he's having a bad dream. If he can't comfort his son, he can at least comfort Billy. He puts his arms around him. The boy doesn't wake. 'It's okay,' he whispers. 'Everything's okay.'

Steam mists the mirrors, slicks every surface. Billy is down on his knees, taking Jack in his mouth. Billy's glistening body is shell-rose in the morning light. He is a beautiful merman from an old mariner's tale - *his hair is silver-blond, his skin is pale as pearl* - luring a landlubber to his doom.

Jack rests his hands on the boy's head, concentrating on the shiny cap of blond hair as he finds his rhythm. The cascade of hot water splashes down over Jack's shoulders, over his chest and abdomen, finding its way to Billy.

Billy.

Billy takes his lips away just before the moment of Jack's oblivion and Jack watches the water wash his semen from the boy's beatific face.

The water is still dripping from the shower head, tap-tap-tap on the tiled floor as they dry each other with fleecy towels fresh from the linen cupboard and Jack imagines every day like this - instead of going for a run to avoid having sex with his wife.

At least he has this now, at least he has Billy, for now;

his peculiar boy, as if borrowed or stolen from another world.

'I want you to stay,' Jack tells him.

'I'd like that.' Billy's eyes are brilliantly, asymmetrically blue in the sunlight. At this moment, Jack sees him for what he really is - a sweet, trusting boy; guileless like a child.

In this moment, in this light, he's nothing like the boy who strips off in broad daylight and begs a grown man to fuck him.

iv

Tea is served in a random assortment of mugs with pictures of Miss Piggy, London Bridge and Hawaiian girls in grass skirts. The greasy spoon on Leytonstone High Road claims 'the best fry-up in east London'. It's a well-worn rest stop for taxi drivers and locals: Formica tables, brown panelled walls, nonstop radio. *Victim of Love* fades into *Misfit* and *So Emotional* and on and on.

After legendary and mountainous fry-ups they go to Billy's flat to collect a few of his things. 'I really like your car, Jack,' Billy says, running his hands along the red leather upholstery of the BMW E12. 'It's like you - sensible, conventional, but a little bit racy underneath.'

Jack winks back at him, saying nothing. The car is getting old now. It was Jack's expensive boy toy back in the day but Lizzie always disapproved, not least because she was pregnant when he bought it. 'We can't afford a mortgage *and* a car loan with a baby on the way.' Jack's beamer was his one last indulgence, a last shout to souped-up cars and Club 18-30 holidays and banter with the lads. The E12 was his rebound lover, a knee-jerk reaction to an impending life of nappy-changing, wet wipes and parents' evenings.

On the other hand, Lizzie fantasised about spending to impress the mums in her social circle - a timeshare in Greece or a weekend place in Dorset, perhaps. She wanted to have something up her sleeve when the dinner party talk turned to husbands' five-figure salaries. That was one of the reasons she wanted Jack to go for a headship. But even then, he'd never earn the kind of money the other husbands did.

And didn't she know it?

Teenage boys in a rag-tag gang - Adidas tracksuits, West Ham shirts - are practising wheelies in the street outside Billy's flat.

'Cool car, mister!' The eldest, and the obvious leader, brings his bike to a skidding halt inches from the front bumper. The rest of the gang follow suit, surrounding the car.

'Thanks,' Jack says, pulling a few coins from his wallet and dropping them into eager palms. 'Keep an eye on it and there's more where that came from when I get back.'

Billy's flatmate is in the living room, flipping through a copy of *Record Mirror*. The boy is good-looking with caramel hair, shaved in close at the sides, and soft brown eyes. His face is beautifully wrought. Billy doesn't introduce him but disappears into his bedroom to pack. Jack sits on a grubby armchair and says, 'I'm Jack.'

'Conor.'

'You're a student too?'

'Yeah.'

'What are you studying?'

'Cultural Studies BA.'

'Sounds interesting.'

'It's all right.' Conor smiles half-heartedly and his face creases in an artless, beguiling way. 'I'm hoping it'll get me some kind of job in the arts,' he says.

'How far are you through the course?'

'Just finished my second year.'

Billy reappears clutching a purple Puma holdall. 'I'm ready,' he says.

Conor goes back to reading his *Record Mirror*.

Billy still doesn't acknowledge him. Billy has been rushing to get his things together so Jack doesn't have too much time in Conor's company. And Jack knows this. Billy is already opening the front door and nodding goodbye to Conor, and Jack sees Billy's eyes flash as he disappears outside.

They drive back home under a furious sun.

And there's Nigel standing by the front door of Claia Bourne. 'Hey, Jack. You feeling better, old son?' Nigel stares at Billy as he gets out of the car with a mixture of curiosity and surprise.

'Not really. My back's still sore.' Jack flicks a thumb at Billy. 'But I needed to go over a few final bits and pieces with Andy here. He's the probationer starting in September.' Jack is praying - as in beseeching God - that Billy will go along with it.

Billy glances at Jack dubiously, then sticks out his hand to Nigel. 'Pleased to meet you.'

'Likewise,' says Nigel.

'I can't wait to get started. And I'm so looking forward to working hard, under Jack.'

Jack makes a performance of rubbing his back and wincing.

'Hot water bottle, then ice,' Nigel says.

They stand uncomfortably on the doorstep like three schoolboys waiting to ask the same girl for a dance. Nigel breaks the deadlock.

'I just came round to see how you were. Lizzie rang and said you were laid up and not able to go away so Sandie issued one of her royal commands, told me to get round here and keep you company.'

'I don't think I'll be much company at the minute,' Jack says.

'Okay.' Nigel backs away like a snitch leaving a couple of gangsters. 'Give me a bell if you change your mind.'

Billy cuffs Jack lightly on the back of the head as he shuts the front door. 'How's your back?'

'Sorry about that. That was my headteacher's husband. Thanks for playing along.'

'Does this little pretence of yours mean we have to stay in the house the whole time? Like, you can't be seen with me?'

'No. We just have to be careful.'

'You really are a very good liar.'

Billy tosses his bag on the floor and hooks his fingers through Jack's belt loops, pulling him in for a lingering kiss. 'Jack, if you told me now you wanted to fuck my brains out...'

'Yeah?'

'You wouldn't be lying, would you?'

They sit in the window, not saying much, watching bedraggled
Saturday shoppers hurry towards the Underground.

chapter four

'BIGOTS CHARTER SAILS THROUGH HOUSE OF LORDS'
Despite minor changes in wording, Clause 28 of the Local Government Bill banning the 'promotion' of homosexuality remains the most vicious assault this century on the civil liberties of gay men and lesbians... The Clause now states that 'a local authority shall not intentionally promote homosexuality or publish material with the intention of promoting homosexuality'. And local authorities shall not 'promote the teaching in any maintained school of the acceptability of homosexuality as a pretended family relationship'.
GAY TIMES, MARCH 1988

i

I couldn't sleep. I was sweltering in the dark, wrong inside with guilt - like a churchgoer who'd stumbled on a nudist colony - and liked it.

Mind wide awake: here I was playing house with a boy

I hardly knew, playing at being someone I wasn't. Playing. Here's what I really was: a liar. No scruples. Decency swept away by desire. Billy had given me an itch and the more I scratched it, the more I liked it, and the more it itched.

ii

Billy places his hand over Jack's hand, lacing his fingers between Jack's fingers. Jack knows it's the most natural thing in the world. For Billy. But not for him. He fights the urge to shift in his seat and pull his hand away. He tells himself to relax. No one's going to see. They've chosen the far end of the back row and the lights are already down. *Hairspray* is starting soon. It's a hot Friday afternoon and there are only three other people in the cinema: an old guy in a flasher mac, and two women, lesbians in all likelihood.

The rest of London is at work or out in the city's parks basking in the sunshine. Jack concentrates on slowing his breathing. Then he squeezes Billy's hand in return. He is aware of the boy turning his head, leaning across and pecking him on the cheek. Jack stares straight ahead at the screen, now a deep ocean blue with white geometric shapes moving to the Pearl and Dean music: *Ba-ba, ba-ba, ba-ba, ba-ba, bubba-baaaaah… bup!*

When they come out of the cinema, the daylight is dazzling. They weave their way through the crowds in Oxford Street. Billy wants to go to the London Lesbian and Gay Centre. Jack's never been. Billy seems to think it's a great place, an antidote to the bar and club scene. It's not yet rush hour so they take the Underground to Farringdon.

The London Lesbian and Gay Centre occupies an old meat warehouse on Cowcross Street. To Jack, it seems like any other municipal space - bland, soulless. Offices and meeting rooms give on to unremarkable, whitewashed corridors. Cork pinboards offer details of advice lines and support groups, everything from legal aid to lesbian yoga.

They order a couple of quiches and some drinks and find a table outside on the terrace, overlooking the nearby train and tube tracks. Billy says he might volunteer at the centre a couple of nights a week, maybe answering the phones.

'This government is out to get us,' he says, stabbing at a shred of browning lettuce. 'Clause 28 is victimisation. We've got to stop them.'

'Our school got some info through from the LEA. The local government act already says sex education should encourage the value of family life. But the LEA's looking at the impact of the new clause. They'll come up with recommendations soon.'

'Jill Knight started the whole thing off. Bitch!' Billy spits unexpectedly. 'She says it's about protecting children. She never shuts up. But it's an enabling act. That's what we reckon.'

'We?'

'The lesbian and gay society at poly. What the government really wants to do with Clause 28 is shut down gay life, stop councils giving licences to bars and clubs, stop funding for places like this. Stop. Stop. Stop. We've got to stop Thatcher, stop all those bastards. We're being trodden on. We're under siege. They just make shit up about us.' His chest is rising and falling and the words are coming faster and louder. 'Thatcher said children are being taught they have an *inalienable right to be gay*. Now she's admitted she's got no evidence to back it up.'

'I remember that speech.' Jack is careful to keep his tone gentle, mollifying. 'It's just politics, Billy. They make stuff up all the time.'

Billy kicks back in his chair, flushing with anger. 'They're a bunch of complete cunts, the whole bloody lot of them.' For a while, neither of them speaks then Billy asks, 'Did you go on the march in February?'

'No, I didn't.'

'We hired a minibus to go up to Manchester.'

'Oh.'

'We all need to take action.'

'I know that. I don't agree with what they're doing either but there are other ways to fight them.'

Jack glances around to make sure no one else can hear him. 'I can't exactly tell my wife I'm going on a gay march.' He thinks Billy is going to launch into another tirade - a hundred reasons why that's exactly what he should do - but Billy's arms are tightly folded. His face is like fury. He shifts slightly in his chair as he looks at Jack.

Then his expression softens. Just like that.

Click.

'Sorry. I get carried away sometimes. Too passionate. Didn't your school organise anything? I know the NUT marched in Manchester.'

'No. We didn't organise anything. It's tricky. Some members of staff support Clause 28.'

Bull. Red rag.

'They must be fucking Nazis!'

'I don't think you can call them Nazis, Billy.'

'That's what they are! Fucking Nazi cunts! What bloody

64

right have they got to tell us how to live?'

Click.

Things are wilder this time. Billy's voice is rising insanely. 'They should be put up against a wall and fucking shot.'

Jack waits for this second fire to burn itself out.

Billy studies his glass of vodka and orange. 'Aren't you tired, Jack? Aren't you tired of lying to everyone, tired of lying to yourself? Don't you want to be free?'

'It's not that straightforward.'

'If you could go back in time, wouldn't you do things differently?'

'I honestly don't know.'

The evening sky is broken pewter, cracked by lightning. Now rain tumbles out of the howling clouds. When the storm finally passes, the tube platforms beyond Stratford are black and silver with pooling water.

iii

Next morning Jack sleeps late again. Hours of sex on top of end-of-term fatigue. He turns his head groggily to the open door. Billy appears with a tray: instant coffee and marmite-on-toast. He is naked except for his red briefs. Except they're not his. Jack realises Billy's wearing Lizzie's red lace panties.

'Here you are gorgeous,' Billy says.

Jack is aroused and horrified. 'What the hell are you doing?'

'Oh, these?' Billy looks down. The lacy underwear has

made him hard. 'I thought you'd like them on me. I look better in them than she does, don't I?'

'Take them off.'

'I could wank in them,' Billy says, 'or you could put them on your face, and do me.' Jack stares at him. 'Come on, Jack. It's just playing.' Billy stands at the side of the bed. Hard. Pouting. Defiant. Swaying slightly. Magnificent. Furious. Hot.

Billy.

'Just take them off, Billy,' Jack says slowly. Lizzie's panties are already damp with Billy's pre-cum. 'For Christ's sake, you shouldn't mess about with other people's stuff.'

Billy stands very still. He says nothing. His eyes are fixed on Jack. One eye seems much, much bluer than the other. He is full of a beautiful, terrible fury. Now he is fury incarnate, visited on Jack from another world. The tray slams into the floor. Billy rips off the panties freeing his furious, glistening erection. He slings the ruined panties at Jack like an angry chimp slinging shit.

'Fuck it, Jack,' he says, glowering, 'you don't have to be so bloody vanilla all the time.'

'I'm not bloody vanilla, I just don't like you wearing my wife's fucking underwear.'

Billy takes Jack's erection carefully in his hands. 'But I think you do.'

They are facing each other now, facing each other down. Jack sighs and lowers his gaze; he wants this storm to pass, too. 'I don't want to argue about it.' He looks at Billy, then at the tray on the floor. 'Specially after such a lovely breakfast on the floor.'

Click.

Now Billy is an eager child given a gold star.

He climbs onto the bed next to Jack. 'You've got nice hairy armpits,' Billy says.

iv

It's an hour or so before they get out of bed and shower. Billy clears up in the kitchen. When Jack finally gets downstairs, he finds Billy in the study, leafing through *Bright Ideas Maths Activities*. Billy puts it back on the shelf and picks up a letter. 'Mr. J. Huntley, Deputy Headteacher, Roughton Road Primary School,' he reads out loud. 'That's where you headed off to after we fucked that first time?'

'Yes. It is.'

Jack takes the letter from him and returns it purposefully to the pile on his desk. His desk is a mess. Billy has been rifling through his papers and Jack thinks to himself that their worlds weren't supposed to mix like this.

Then he finds himself thinking about the storm last night, the thunder clouds extending high into the sky over London in great towers and plumes. *Cumulonimbus* is the word: dark, wall-like, shaped like an anvil where the top of the cloud has hit its head on the troposphere.

v

Billy fiddles about with mousse, pulling Jack's hair this way and that, to give him what he says is a feathered, 'sexier' look. As the boy's fingers circle his scalp, Jack feels himself getting hard again. He could take the boy to bed all week, and still come back for more.

67

When he looks in the mirror, he has to admit it's an improvement. It's taken a few years off him, made him look more 'with it'.

Now Billy wants to go to the Photographers' Gallery. The weather is still unsettled. Rain pitter-patters on and off like a leaky tap as they wander through Covent Garden. The piazza is overrun with tourists drawn by the *Shop Assistance* jazz festival in aid of the Terrence Higgins Trust. The exhibition at The Photographers' Gallery turns out to be *Behold the Man*, a collection of photographs of men. Naked.

All eyes seem to be on Jack and Billy as they make their way into the exhibition (the gallery seems full of gay couples). Jack is more used to darkened basement bars and his face feels hot as he moves quickly around the brightly lit room. He loses Billy, somehow, in the crowd and hurries through the exhibition alone. He has more than one reason to hurry; the models in the pictures are astonishingly sexy, 'real beauties' as Warhol would have put it; Jack is used to looking at naked boys alone and in private, not in a crowded room. Buttocks. Balls. Cock. Silently, he counts backwards from a thousand to stave off another wave of arousal.

Drizzle has settled in for the rest of the day. They sit in the window at Pizzaland, not saying much, watching bedraggled Saturday shoppers hurry towards the Underground. Jack's unease at the gallery (*Buttocks. Balls. Cock.*) has cast a shadow over the afternoon.

He digs into his wallet and hands the waitress a 'pizza

for a penny' coupon.

Jack and Billy work their way through two overcooked Hawaiian deep crusts, loaded with pineapple, ham and mozzarella. Billy seems to cheer up as his belly gets fuller. Jack suggests they go on to The Bell in King's Cross; a dark smoky palace with a mixed clientele - much easier - no art - completely anonymous.

They squeeze into a spot by the crowded dance floor, Jack struggling now with the effects of his third pint of Carlsberg as *Chains of Love* starts to play.

'I love this one!' Billy shouts over the music. 'Let's dance.' Before Jack knows what's happening, Billy pulls him into the whirling rabble. Billy is pressed up against him. They aren't really dancing; it's impossible in the closely-packed crowd; their bodies rub together in time to the music. Jack would have been uneasy dancing with another man, even in a gay bar, but he is drunk, unshackled by the liberating effects of the alcohol. Everything is fluid now. It's all an experiment, a careless fiction. No harm done.

Billy puts his arms around Jack's shoulders and now Jack is kissing him. Now the song changes to *Set Me Free* and they are pressed against a pillar; Jack's arms tight around the boy; Jack's tongue in the soft recesses of Billy's mouth. Jack is hard. A juggernaut. His dick is pulsing, oozing and Jaki Graham's words are hammering in his head and a couple of leather-clad muscle men are watching and stroking each other and getting off, and Jack is surfing. Higher. And higher.

(*Buttocks. Balls. Cock.*)

And, for a moment, he thinks he might pass out.

He takes Billy outside and the drizzle is falling steadily and he manages to convince a reluctant cabbie to take them out to Westward Hatch. They hold hands in the back of the cab and Jack is reckless with desire now like an inexperienced adolescent boy. No more a slave to 'normality'. (*Buttocks. Balls. Cock.*) He is free. He can't remember how much it costs but he remembers giving the driver a bunch of notes.

He throws Billy onto the bed in the guest room. He is light-headed, struggling with his tee shirt, arms tangled over his head. He looks down and sees his own cock tenting his black briefs. Billy slips off the bed, naked and wide-eyed. 'Come and get me,' he says. And then he is gone. Jack stumbles out of his underwear. The light is burning in the master bedroom. Billy is stretched out on the bed, laughing. Through the haze, Jack hesitates. This is the room he shares with Lizzie. This is the bed he shares with Lizzie. Billy pats the space beside him impatiently. 'Come on, green eyes. What are you waiting for?'

'I sleep in this bed with my wife.'

Billy is staring up at him. 'Do you love her?'

'No.' Jack is hammered. He can't stop the truth from finding its way out.

'Come on then.'

Jack climbs onto the bed. Billy cups Jack's balls as they kiss.

vi

Bells are ringing. I'm running up to the porch of the church. I've been trying to get to the wedding for hours. Now I'm

70

impossibly late. All heads turn to look at me as I stumble through the doors: men in neatly-pressed suits, women in wide-brimmed hats with bows, feathers and flowers. I can't quite make out their faces. Perhaps they are faceless. I am dripping in sweat; my dress shirt clings to me and my morning coat is torn at the elbow. Lizzie is at the altar, veil lifted, eyes red-rimmed from crying. She flings her bouquet on the floor and coral rose petals scatter. She yells at me through her sobs, 'You bastard! You've ruined everything! Bastard!' The bells are intolerable. They ring and they ring and they ring.

vii

Jack opens his eyes and they hurt. The phone by the bed is ringing. He picks it up.

'Jack?'

He sits up too quickly, head like a stone on the fragile stick of his neck. He grimaces and shuts his eyes again.

'Hey, Lizzie,' he croaks, 'you okay?' His voice is a husky bass from too much drink, too much smoke.

'I was going to ask you that.' She sounds pissed off. 'I rang four times last night. And I rang this morning.' Severely pissed off. 'What's going on? Where have you been?'

Jack tries to remember when he spoke to her last. Yesterday afternoon sometime it must have been, just before he and Billy went out. He didn't think she'd ring again so soon. He hadn't thought to check the machine. All he's been thinking about is sex with Billy. Sex. Billy. Sex. Billy. He looks over his shoulder, expecting to see the boy there. The bed is empty.

'Jack?' Lizzie says again.

71

'I'm still here.'

'So, where have you been?'

'I haven't been anywhere, baby. I took some painkillers. The strong ones the doc gave me for my back. They knocked me out.'

'For God's sake, Jack. I thought something had happened. I rang Nigel and Sandie. Nigel offered to go over this morning.'

'Tell him not to!' Jack realises this is too much. 'I mean, tell him there's really no need. Honestly, I'm fine. Feeling a lot better.'

Silence at the other end of the line, then, 'I'm glad. What are you doing this afternoon?'

'This afternoon?' He looks at the clock. It's 1pm. 'I dunno,' he says, 'potter around, read the paper.'

'Did you manage to get to the bank?'

Shit.

'I wasn't feeling up to it,' he says sheepishly.

'You could have done it on Thursday when you had the new guy over from school.'

Andy – Billy – Andy – Billy

'I'll do it tomorrow morning. I'll be back to normal by then, I'm sure.'

Silence again.

'Okay. I'll see you tomorrow,' she says. 'Thomas is looking forward to seeing his daddy.'

'I can't wait to see you both.'

Jack sits for a while, pressing the handset firmly against his forehead to dull the ache. What if Nigel turns up at the house? *Billy.*

Nigel is a no-nonsense, down-to-earth 'good bloke'. He

72

works as an accountant for Midland Bank in Leyton Green; has done his entire career. He preferred it that way; same people, same routines, nothing out of the ordinary. Nothing to upset the applecart. He liked his pipe and his slippers and his Sunday supplements. He liked his tennis matches with Jack; 'a younger bloke to keep me on my toes'. If Nigel ever had a fire in his belly, it kindled and flared on the hardcourt and only there.

In the Bateson household, it was Sandie who 'wore the trousers'. It was Sandie who had the real drive and ambition. Nigel and Sandie had married young, had kids within a couple of years and he'd expected her to be the homemaker.

But Sandie wasn't the stay-at-home kind. As soon as the boys were in nursery school, she'd swiped a hefty chunk of Nigel's salary, hired a nanny and enrolled to study for a B Ed. Her graduation photo stood proudly on the mantelpiece. She hotfooted her way from class teacher to deputy to headship. She told Jack her next stop was head of the local authority education department.

Jack had encouraged Nigel to set up on his own, work freelance, build up his own business, escape the nine-to-five. But Nigel had never been the kind to break away from the herd. That didn't mean he wasn't envious of anyone who did. Envy could make him a little caustic at times but Jack liked Nigel. Nigel was so reassuringly normal. He enjoyed his company. Normal Nigel. He enjoyed playing tennis and going down the pub. Normal. But sometimes he wondered quite what Sandie saw in Nigel.

Jack sniffs the bedsheets: musk, cum. They'll have to go into the wash before the 'fish and chips' get back. He pulls on a pair of pyjama bottoms and goes in search of Billy. The boy is at the breakfast table, spooning rubbery scrambled eggs onto scorched toast.

'Hey, sleepyhead. I was about to come and get you.'

Jack finds it hard to look at Billy for a moment. He's just been lying to his wife and it was so easy - like golden syrup falling off a warm spoon. Jack may be the one sinner who cannot be saved. *Hallelujah!* He has spent the night fucking this boy in his marital bed. Now, come the morning, he's on the telephone telling sweet lies to his wife. *Amen!*

'I had the best time last night,' Billy says as he pours the tea into mugs. He holds the spout high, watching the stream of brown liquid falling down, like a child at the water tray.

'You're full of beans this morning,' Jack says.

'It's afternoon.'

'I was forgetting.'

'I found some Alka-Seltzer in the bathroom cabinet. I had the last two. Sorry. Didn't think you'd need them, being such a big, tough, married man.'

'Thanks for making breakfast. I don't know how much I can manage.'

Jack is thinking about Lizzie and Thomas and the family breakfast eaten every morning in this kitchen. It's a comfortable routine, and comforting to think about it: Lizzie, the expert cook, serving up the perfect fried breakfast; eggs with soft runny yolks, sunny side up; crisp

74

rashers of bacon; rich, pulpy fried tomatoes; thick slices of fried bread. Instinctively, Jack looks over to the picture of Lizzie and Thomas on the window sill - except it's not there. The frame is the same but the picture inside is different. *Billy.* 'What's this?'

'The person you really love,' Billy says, blushing slightly. Jack tries to open the back of the frame.

'Come on, Jack,' Billy says, 'just for today, just while we're together.'

'Where's the other photo, Billy?' Now he is the teacher bringing the wayward child to heel.

Billy fishes the picture out of the bin. It was taken in Spain: a lurid, overstuffed hotel lobby in Madrid. Lizzie is sitting with Thomas on her lap. He is resting his head sleepily on her shoulder, looking supremely sorry for himself. Jack remembered the journey out, the plane delayed for five or six hours; Thomas ready for a nuclear tantrum by the time they reached the Palace Hotel.

Jack had always appreciated Lizzie's ability to calm Thomas down in situations like that. She focused her attention only on him. She held him and steadied him with her concentration and the sound of her voice.

By contrast Jack was the court jester, the one who geed his son up, playing games and goofing around. Lizzie always knew exactly what to do when Thomas was struggling in the world. The photo captured perfectly a golden moment. Thomas must have been just five years old. Now the picture is smeared with grease and broken eggshells. Jack snatches it from Billy and wipes it carefully with a kitchen towel.

'It's a bloody stupid thing to do,' he snaps.

Billy frowns. 'I thought you'd want a picture of me in

the house. You told me you don't love your wife. You said it last night. Why don't you just fucking leave her?'

'I was drunk last night, Billy.'

'So, you *do* love her, then?'

Jack looks out towards the garden, unwilling to say anything more. Billy puts his hands on his hips. 'No,' he says triumphantly, 'you *don't* love her, do you?'

'It's not as simple as that.'

'I'd have thought it was perfectly simple. Why don't you stop lying? You'll be a million times happier. Don't you owe it to yourself? Don't you owe it to *her*? She might prefer to be with a guy who actually *wants* to stick his dick in her.'

Jack moves towards Billy. The boy stands his ground.

'I'm not going to discuss this with you, Billy. It's none of your business.'

'None of my business? How many times have you fucked me in the last few days? More times than you've fucked your wife in months!'

'Shut up!' Jack's fists are clenched at his sides. Billy's face blanches and then he begins to cry. He throws his arms around Jack and sobs, his whole body shuddering.

Click.

'I'm sorry, Jack,' Billy whispers, looking up into Jack's eyes. His face is pale as pearl, wet with tears. 'I don't want us to fight like this. I just said those things because I care so much about you.' He pauses. 'You're the One, Jack.' He pauses again. 'I love you.'

Jack holds him by the shoulders, keeping him at arm's length. 'You're a great kid, Billy. But you don't love me, and we're *not* in a relationship. We can't be.'

'Yes we can! We can build a life together, Jack. You can

76

be free. I can help you.'

'No!' Billy is suffocating him; his marriage is suffocating him; life is suffocating him.

Billy wipes his nose with the back of his hand. 'Tell me I don't mean anything to you. Tell me you don't love me.'

'This was only ever supposed to be a bit of fun. Remember? You said so yourself. A fling.'

'That's not true.' Billy puts his fingers over Jack's mouth to stop the words.

Jack pushes him away firmly. 'I like you Billy. I really do. But I *don't* love you.'

'Liar!' Billy yells at him.

The garden at Claia Bourne is large and Jack's pretty sure the neighbours can't hear but he closes the open window anyway.

'That's right,' Billy spits, 'protect your precious reputation. Your precious little lie of a life.'

Jack breathes deeply. 'I think you'd better go.'

'No, Jack. Please!' Jack pushes him away again.

'I want you to go, Billy. Now.'

They stare at each other for a long moment.

'Fine.'

Jack hears him stamping upstairs, slamming doors, getting his things.

'If you wait a minute,' Jack says, 'I'll get some clothes on and drive you to the station. We can talk on the way.'

'Go to hell!'

I am carrying Billy. We are fleeing. Our faces and clothes are filthy because we haven't washed in days.

chapter five

i

I went through drawers and cupboards, through stacks of neatly-ironed tee shirts and work shirts, pulling apart bundles of socks and underwear, looking for anything that Billy might have left behind, unwittingly or deliberately, to betray me to my wife.

I found nothing.

I stripped the beds and put the washing machine on. I ran myself a bath. My hangover kicked in like a blunt instrument to the back of the head. I found a packet of aspirin six months out of date but took a couple anyway, washing them down with a can of Coke. I belched loudly.

It was good to be alone.

I eased into the hot water and closed my eyes. The hot bathwater relaxed my muscles. The pain behind my eyes became less insistent. I lay back and pictured Billy - on the Central Line by now probably, heading back to Stratford, back to his own world of bars and clubs and gay interest groups and kids who were just like him.

I am kissing Billy at The Bell. The two muscle men are ogling us, getting off on our sex. We were the show and they were the hungry voyeurs. Imagine if we had asked them back to the house for a no-holds-barred performance: Billy naked underneath me; the pale downy hairs around his navel, his cock hard, his nipples thick and rubbery; his boyish face and white-blond hair; the little silver necklace that dangles from his slim throat.

I open my eyes. My erection is floating on the line of soapy water like a ship anchored at low tide. I pool some shower gel into my palm and work it over my dick, closing my fist around the shaft. Now my hand is working up and down. Now I am back in the moment with Billy, licking his nipples as he strokes my hard-on. He is teasing the foreskin with practised fingers, euphoric, the sweet and trusting boy I need him to be, regardless of the reality. He tickles my nipples with his thumbs and my cock pulses. I am on my back and he is on top of me and he is taking both our hard-ons in his slick hand, rubbing them together. I take hold of his young supple butt and he sits back on me, my hardness slipping easily into the warmth of him.

My body is tense in rigid anticipation, thighs pressed so hard against the tub, red weals rise on my skin. Now I am shooting white ribbons. My body surrenders, spasms and relaxes, gratified; I breathe steadily again. I look down to see the long elastic strands floating just under the surface of the water. I stand up and the semen congeals on my stomach and legs. I towel myself off and roll the towel up and place it carefully at the bottom of the laundry basket.

ii

Sunlight streamed into the study, casting bright diamonds over my desk. I worked my way through a pile of invitations: our wedding anniversary, ten glorious years. I addressed envelopes with the Mont Blanc Lizzie gave me last birthday. Writing took my mind off things, returned life to normality. Lizzie would be glad I'd made headway with the list. But I was also careful not to deprive her - she derived a masochistic pleasure from domestic martyrdom; there was always too much shopping to do, too many charity lunches; not enough housekeeping allowance. I stopped slightly less than half way through the list so there would be plenty for her still to write. She'd be pleased with me and the happier she was, the less inclined she'd be to ask awkward questions.

The late afternoon breeze murmured dolefully through the trees. Here's where Billy lay down in the grass at the edge of the golf course. Here's where Billy pulled down his jeans. Here's where Billy Soanes asked me to fuck him.
Billy.
Billy was gone now. I'd never see him again. I tried to imagine him older, old. I should have handled it

differently, handled him differently. I'd led him on and I knew it.

With Billy everything was black and white. Everything was charged with youthful indignation. His idealism was seeded and watered, no doubt, in corners of the students' union: *young and naïve Billy*. He wanted sex in the long grass at the back of the house. He wanted to hold hands and kiss in public: *young and reckless Billy*. He'd thrown my wife and kid in the rubbish and replaced them with himself: *young and spiteful Billy*.

But there was no denying I was at fault. I had asked him to stay at Claia Bourne. I had let him get used to our being together, playing house. I'd done it all because I wanted to. No one had coerced me. I wanted to experiment with another life. He had been my guinea pig. I wanted to see what happened when I turned the flame up high. I was the one who told him I didn't love my wife. I was the one who fucked him in the bed where she and I usually slept. I'd played a game with him. He was just a kid; but I should have known better.

Walking helped to put some emotional distance between me and the trauma of Billy.

I thought a beer or two at The Rose and Crown might help as well, and it certainly wouldn't do any harm. I drank my pint and had another and contemplated my return to family life. Lizzie would set off early tomorrow. She'd complain good-naturedly about my messiness. She'd tidy obsessively. She'd count the number of empty takeaway cartons. By teatime, it would be like she'd never been away. Part of me was looking forward to seeing her. Part of me felt a familiar sinking feeling. My spirits rose when I thought about my son. I'd promised to take Thomas out on Wednesday and I was looking forward to planning something nice for him. I'd also promised him a few tennis lessons to see if I couldn't mould him into the next Björn Borg. You never know.

It was dusk when I strolled home, relaxed and light-headed after the couple of lagers. I'd hardly eaten anything all day but I couldn't face another takeaway. I made myself beans on toast and sprawled in front of the TV with another lager (what the hell!) and watched Moviedrome.

I'd seen *Invasion of the Body Snatchers* when I was a kid; mum let me stay up late after I'd worn her down with my relentless pleading. I knew the film was often regarded as a comment on McCarthyism but for me it took on a new, particular meaning. The emotionless body snatchers were the people around me in the lie of a life I'd chosen for myself. They had no idea who I really was underneath my own false skin. Lizzie, her parents, Sandie, Nigel were all part of a collective way of life alien to me. Slowly but surely, their influence had overtaken me. I had been invaded. My body had been taken over. My life had been snatched. Did anyone ever escape? The future looked like a blind alley full of piss and broken bottles.

iii

Into the dark archway of a road bridge. I stumble through a filthy smear of mud. I am carrying Billy. Our faces and clothes are filthy; we haven't washed in days. I have to stop, if only for a moment, to rest. I lower Billy to the ground, tenderly.

83

His eyes are closed. I see the beauty of the boy caught in the hopeless tangle of sleep. I kiss him for what I know must be the final time. His eyes slowly open.

'There's no way out for you, Jack,' he whispers. 'Stop fighting it. Become one of us.'

'I can't.' I back away from him.

'Then I guess They can have you.' He shouts at our pursuers, 'He's in here! Come and get him!' His face is full of a pent-up fury I recognise all too well. And now I am running across meadows streaked with mist. Deeper and deeper I run into the night. And I am terribly afraid. The boy I let into my life is the architect of my ruin, a sybaritic Trojan horse.

I see lights ahead – a road? – and I start to run faster. And I'm getting nowhere.

Now they are coming for me: my friends, my family, my workmates. Their faces are inhuman in the half-light. They will rip me to shreds in their righteous anger.

'Liar!' Lizzie is screaming. 'Bastard fucking liar!'

The lights in the distance are headlights, cars backed up in interminable lines, crawling, crawling; early evening rush hour on the North Circular road. Maybe someone will stop and help me get away. If I can get far enough away, maybe I can forget, maybe we can all forget.

Something small – a deer, a sheep I think at first – moves just ahead, coming out of the dark, into the glare of the headlights.

'Daddy!' Thomas is sobbing. Disconsolate in the light. Afraid.

I pick him up. Now my pursuers have vanished but they have already won. Billy is standing in their place, oddly incandescent with glee.

Billy.

'You'll never ever be free. The truth always comes out. It's your turn, Jack. You're next!'

I started awake. In the liminal space between waking and sleep, the light struck me as sinful, sinning. Terrible images appeared in my mind's eye - the King's Cross fire, the Japan Air Lines disaster, the gruesome killings on the Cornish lighthouse, *Devil's Rock*.

I went up to bed and found it unmade. I fished around in the laundry cupboard, found the wrong size sheets, cursed, fished again. By the time I was done, it was late. I sank into bed ready to sleep the sleep of the dead. But I woke up again, boiling hot and insanely thirsty. Every hour on the hour, or at least it seemed that way. I guzzled water from the tap, and still it did nothing to satisfy my thirst.

iv

In the morning, my shame returned and I was sickened all over again by what I'd done behind my wife's back. The alarm read: 9.23am. I pictured Lizzie, already on the road, Thomas strapped in beside her, Simon Mayo's Breakfast Show blaring from tinny speakers against the roar of the motorway outside. The distance between them and me was shrinking fast.

I shaved quickly, cursing as I nicked myself in my hurry. I took a shower and got dressed. I made up the guest room with clean sheets and did one last paranoid sweep of the house to make sure no telltale sign remained of sex - *Billy cups Jack's balls as they kiss* - with Billy.

I felt an odd, nervous excitement; how far away is Lizzie now? I was racing against the clock, covering my tracks. I drove down to Midland Bank and settled the bloody gas bill. I went to the supermarket and bought flowers. Something to keep Lizzie sweet. I still had enough time to get home, steel my nerves with a Scotch, stay my guilt, put my shame away in a box with a tight lid, and loosen up before she marched upstairs and unpacked in the bedroom where I'd fucked Billy.

Billy cups Jack's balls as they kiss.

Lizzie's Fiesta was already in the driveway when I got home. My time had run out. I hadn't been this nervous since our wedding night.

Thomas came bounding towards me and I squeezed him tight and swung him round and he babbled about the things he'd seen: rabbits and deer in the woodlands at Padley Gorge; the New York street and Check Point Charlie on the Granada studio tour, and then there was Lizzie, harassed as usual.

'Where've you been?'

'I went to pay that bill,' I said, 'and I got you these.'

She brightened momentarily as she smelled the dozen red roses. 'They're beautiful.' Then she eyed me dubiously. 'You never buy me flowers.'

'That's not true.'

'All right. You never buy me flowers without a hint.'

'I missed you.' I kissed her and I felt nothing but shame. Shame, and the familiar glass wall between us.

I was out of my body, looking down on a stranger, looking down on a woman in the stranger's arms. 'How was the trip back?'

She groaned.

Billy cups Jack's balls as they kiss.

'Fine until we hit the M25. Why are there hardly any services on that bloody motorway? Of course, this one was bursting to go.' She thumbed at Thomas and he looked suitably hangdog. 'I had to pull onto the hard shoulder.'

I heaved her cases from the boot and carried them inside. Thomas was already racing up the stairs to his room, eager to dig out whatever toy had caught his scampering imagination.

'Don't run in the house,' Lizzie shouted after him. I took the luggage upstairs and Lizzie flopped down on the bed, kicking off her shoes. 'Come here,' she said. She reached up and pulled me down on top of her. 'I forgot to say, I missed you too, handsome.' Thomas's footsteps sounded on the landing and I rolled off her. He was holding up an Airfix kit.

'Can I do my Spitfire model downstairs?'

'Sure,' I said. 'I'll come and help you in a minute.'

'Make sure you put newspaper out,' Lizzie told him. 'I don't want glue all over the table.'

She was in the bathroom now, emptying her toiletry bag and putting things back in the right place.

'Jack?'

I found her standing in front of the cabinet, the door wide open. 'What's this, darling?'

How had I overlooked the bottle of mousse? I'd checked over and over for anything of Billy's - his Insignia, his hairbrush, his toothbrush - the mousse had been staring me in the face the whole time.

My mind raced. 'Didn't you ask me to get it for you a while back?'

'No, I don't think so.' She looked at me oddly. 'And it's been used. It's half empty.'

'Then I've been diddled.' I put on my most engaging grin. I heard Thomas calling from downstairs and I hurried off, leaving Lizzie staring after me.

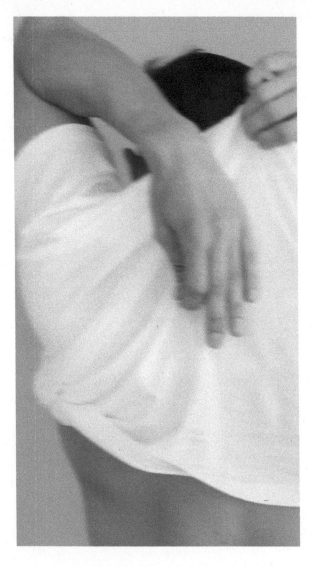

I smiled and took off my top.
The cotton murmured against my skin.

chapter six

i

Thomas's eyes kept closing no matter how hard he tried to stay awake. I closed *Rebecca's World*, kissed him gently on the forehead and smoothed down his bedclothes. I turned on the night light and quietly closed the door.

I found Lizzie lying on our bed in black lace panties, no bra.

'I've been waiting for you, Mr Huntley.'

I took off my top. The cotton murmured against my skin. She moved to the edge of the bed and tugged down the waistband of my tracksuit bottoms. Then she took my flaccid prick out of my briefs and sucked it into life with her soft warm mouth.

I pictured Tony from the pages of *Mister*. *Blond, honey-faced. Nipples that are sweet pink nubs. Cock framed by sepia pubes. Playful smile. Sexy boy next door.*

Part of me was glad Lizzie was getting something she wanted. A bigger part of me felt demoralised and trapped.

I was sorry for the position I'd put us both in. I was fucking her but focusing on someone else. I was failing as a husband, and as a man.

Now Lizzie was lying on her back, eyes lifting to meet mine. 'Make love to me.'

I turned her round, kissing her softly on the shoulders as I entered her, doggy-style. I placed one hand firmly on the back of her neck, so she couldn't turn her head to face me. She moaned as I moved in and out of her.

Tony.
Fucking Tony.
In and out.
Tony.
Gliding and sliding.
Tony. Tony.
Pulsing and pistoning.
Tony. Tony. Tony.
Deep inside of Tony.

Lizzie crawled forwards on the bed and I slipped out of her. She turned and pulled me down, and guided me back inside. I buried my face in her neck and kissed her - and that way I didn't have to look her in the eye.

My guilt stood between me and my hard-on.

I changed tack, focusing on myself, on my bestial masculinity. Here was the procreative instinct, a human male seeding his mate.

But it was no good.

I'd fucked Billy so many times in the past few days,

there was nothing left in my aching balls. I wasn't going to come.

'My back's sore again,' I said as I rolled off her. Now she climbed on top of me, taking me inside once more.

I grimaced. 'No, your weight, the pressure's hurting my back.' Lizzie climbed off me again, the moment gone.

'You need to see someone, darling,' she said sullenly. 'Get it sorted out.'

ii

Summer rain had made the ground soft and blood-warm.

The supermarket on the Broadway was busy with office workers and shop assistants in search of lunch. I steadied the shopping trolley as Thomas pushed it just a little too recklessly behind his mother.

Lizzie tossed in fresh vegetables, packets of Sports biscuits (Thomas's favourites), jars of pasta sauce, packets of rice, noodles and cereal.

To make last night's lie credible (one more lie in a great line of lies), I had to cancel the knockabout I'd planned with Nigel. I was fed up and irritable.

Thomas seemed to catch my mood, screwing up his fists and crying uncontrollably when this month's *Detective Comic* was sold out. His disappointment grounded me.

I dropped Lizzie home, unloaded the weekly shop, then took him on a hunt for a copy.

'We're going to find one,' I said as we pulled up outside our fourth newsagent. We were casting our net wider and wider, and Thomas was more inconsolable with each failed attempt. He looked at me hopelessly.

'Bet we won't,' he mumbled.

'Yes, we will. We're on a mission. Batman wouldn't give up, would he?'

'You're not Batman, daddy.'

'How do you know? I might be.' I squeezed his cheek. 'Don't worry. Daddy will find you your comic if he has to fly to the moon to get it.'

Thomas raced inside the shop before I had a chance to lock the car. I found him clutching the prize close to his chest and grinning up at me. His seven-year-old mind had flipped in an instant from hopeless despair to 'best day ever'.

'I told you,' I said, walking him up to the counter. 'Batman to the rescue.'

As we weren't playing tennis, Nigel suggested we sank a few jars together. The pub was pleasant enough, if a little down on its luck. It smelled of ripe hops and damp. An ageing hippy had installed himself at the far end of the bar, holding court with, and selling weed to, a group of teenage boys from Bancroft's, the local private school. I found Nigel in the lounge, a pint of Stella waiting for me.

'I hope your back problem doesn't mean you'll be retiring from *der weiße Sport* for good,' he said.

'No chance,' I told him. 'It's just a blip, probably a trapped nerve or something. Lizzie's managed to get me in at the osteopath tomorrow.'

'We need you back on court as soon as possible,' he said, winking at me. 'You were playing like a girl in that last match.'

'Get lost, I was carrying you most of the time.' I drank

some of my pint. Nigel opened a packet of salt and vinegar crisps.

'Let's hope this osteo sorts you out tomorrow. Maybe you'll get some little dolly bird with big knockers. Watch out you don't get a stiffy when she's rubbing you down.' *Billy cups Jack's balls as they kiss.* 'Just shut your eyes and think of Glenys Kinnock.'

'I'll bear that in mind.'

I changed the subject. 'How's everything with you?'

'Same old, same old, you know,' he said. 'I've ordered a couple of rather large rhododendrons. I was wondering if you'd come round and help me get them in the ground, once your back's sorted?'

'Of course.'

'Suppose you're making the most of your six weeks of freedom. You lucky bleeder. Or is the missus keeping you busy around the house?'

'Bits and pieces. But I get to spend more time with Thomas, which is great and takes the pressure off Lizzie a little.'

'How did you get on with that skinny little streak of piss last week?'

'Who's that?' I said.

(I knew exactly who he meant.)

'That new recruit you're mentoring. The one I saw at your house.'

'Oh, Andy. He's okay.'

'Odd-looking bugger if you ask me.'

'In what way?'

'That bright white hair. Blokes dying their hair. It's

utterly ridiculous.'

'I don't think it's dyed, Nigel.'

'Christ, poor sod. Makes him look like one of those, doesn't it?'

'One of those what?'

Nigel wiggled a limp wrist at me. 'You know. Backs to the wall, lads!'

Billy cups Jack's balls as they kiss.

'I don't follow.'

'Maybe he's into little boys.'

Now there were two of me: the me that wanted to play along, protect myself; and the me that wanted to deck Nigel. 'Let's talk about something else shall we?' I said.

'D'you reckon Edberg will win the US Open again? Make it a double after Wimbledon?'

'Edberg's seeded third. My money's on Wilander. Him and Lendl for the final again.'

Going shirtless would make Ivan Lendl look hot, poll suggests.

'You're probably right. The Swedes know how to knock out a champion or two. Not like our useless lot.'

'I think Navratilova will take the women's title.'

Nigel leaned back and regarded me sceptically. 'She hasn't dominated the US Open as much as she's dominated Wimbledon. Great big bull dyke. Normal girls playing against her...' He paused with a derisive shake of the head.

Martina Navratilova, who admits to being bisexual though her most recent relationships have been with women, says a chief sponsor of women's tennis will pull out if she goes public with her private life.

'What about it?'

'Doesn't seem right. It must be like playing against a bloke.'

Then I lost it. 'She's not a bloody bloke! And she's not a dyke, she's bisexual.'

'Allegedly.'

'For God's sake, Nigel. Are we going to talk about gays and lesbians all night? What's got into you?'

'All right, Jack. Relax!'

iii

'You don't need to get out of the way, my darling,' Nora would tell me with a mischievous gleam in her eyes, 'I'll just dust round you.' But it was always best to leave her to it. Lizzie headed off for brunch at Sandie's. As soon as she was gone, I called the osteopath and cancelled my appointment. Then I took Thomas swimming.

The municipal baths at Barkingside were humid and airless. Changing rooms crowded with dads and sons; a minefield of papilloma virus and naked men. A twenty-something guy strolled up to a locker, hung up his denim jacket, undid his Hawaiian shirt and peeled off his corduroys to reveal blue-and-white striped briefs. As he pushed them down, I saw his cock was uncut.

I looked away and busied myself getting Thomas changed; sliding his water wings onto his arms; tying the drawstring on his swimming shorts; making sure he put everything safely away in his locker. Like the other kids, he hesitated at the walk-through showers, screwing his nose up at the chlorine smell drifting in from the pool. I told him we'd march straight through like big tough soldiers and he squealed, and jumped as the spattering water caught him.

Thomas was getting more confident in the water and I hoped he might even get his ten-metre swimming certificate next term. I led him up and down the shallow end, letting go of him every now and then. He'd look panicked momentarily then splash and struggle towards me. He held his head well back, his back stiffly arched, his hands slapping against the water, determinedly.

Twenty-Something walked towards the deep end, the sheeny material of his red speedos stretching and twisting over his tight butt. He passed a group of kids goofing around, jumping in from the side, dive bombing each other. They watched as he climbed the ladder to the high board. He stood at the edge, arms outstretched, stomach muscles tight, a wet-dream 15th-century saint. He brought his arms up over his head, paused - an agonising pause - then sprang forwards into the air, hugging his knees as he turned two perfect somersaults *right-round, right-round* and straightened his body in perfect time to break cleanly through the surface and re-enter the pool. I watched his taut brown form disappear, narrow-hipped and sharp as a javelin. Seconds later, he surfaced, powered to the side and hauled himself out. Water cascaded down his back and thighs, his red trunks slick in the wavering light from the poolside windows.

'Daddy! Daddy! Look at me!' Thomas was struggling towards me through foamy water, open-mouthed. Just as he reached me he went under and took a mouthful. He stopped, tried to stand up and slipped, dunking himself again. I pulled him up, up into the air, up, holding him up, up tight, safe and sound, *whoops-a-daisy*, but he started to cry.

By the time we got home, Nora had worked her magic for another week. My shirts, socks and trousers were laid out on the bed in neatly folded piles like a display in an expensive clothes store. Lizzie came home ten minutes after us, coming into the ensuite as I was taking a leak.

'Good brunch?' I asked

'Fab.' She showed me a green paisley kaftan. 'Sandie was throwing a load of old stuff out. I asked if I could have this. It's from the sixties. D'you like it? I love it.'

'It'll look great on you.'

'And I volunteered you for the jumble sale next Saturday,' she said as she hung up my shirts and stuffed socks away in my drawer. 'I said you'd do a stint on the door, selling raffle tickets. Only a couple of hours.' I found it hard to conceal my disappointment. I wanted to unwind at the weekend, tidy the garden, clear out some papers from the study. 'How was the osteopath?'

'Fine.' *Stomach muscles tight, a wet-dream 15th-century saint.*

'Will you need to go back?'

'No, all done.'

'What did they say it was?'

'Just some torn muscles, tension in the lower back. Actually, I was feeling better this morning. I almost cancelled.'

Lizzie came up behind me, put her arms around me and kissed the back of my neck. 'You're all tense because you work too hard, baby. Maybe I could give you a back

99

rub later, and we can pick up where we left off?'

'Sounds good.' I would be able to perform tonight, with the help of Tony from *Mister*. Or maybe even if I thought about Billy…

'If I bribe you with tea and biscuits, do you think you could put up the shelves in Thomas's room?'

'Twist my arm.'

Arms outstretched, stomach muscles tight.

The humdrum routine of life with the Huntleys was back with a vengeance. I was bored into insensibility, anaesthetised by routine, so that I became unable to touch or feel the things closest to me. I'd thought about ending it often enough, ending the boredom, blotting myself out for good. A razor blade or a short thick rope. The coward's way out; that's what they called it.

I grabbed my toolbox and brought in the planks of pine from the garage. Thomas wanted to put his Looney Tunes and Ninja Turtle action figures on one shelf and his racing cars on the other. I placed the first bracket in the wall opposite his bed.

Narrow-hipped and sharp as a javelin.

Taking my spirit level, I measured the distance for the next bracket and marked its position.

Water cascaded down his back and thighs.

I drilled into the wall.

I am kissing Tony.

I inserted the Rawlplugs.

I am inside Tony.

I fixed the bracket in place.

Billy is kneeling in front of me.

I slid the shelf onto the brackets, securing it onto the bracket arms from the underside.

Billy is taking me in his mouth. The two muscle men are watching us. Getting off on us. Me and Billy. Billy and me.

I leaned against the wall.

Billy.
Fucking him.
Taking him.
Doing him.

Suddenly Lizzie's voice: 'Brought you tea and biscuits, darling.'

iv

Lizzie was an expert cook. The freedom and the time to try new things was the one thing she really liked about being a stay-at-home mum. I'd eaten a terrific Baked Alaska at a restaurant once, and raved about it, and within a week it was on the table at home. *The way to a man's heart...*

Thomas was a fussy eater, and that got under her skin.

'What's this stuff in it?'

'What stuff?'

'These black bits?'

'It's just a little burnt around the edges.'

'I don't like it.'

Thomas always wanted to get away from the dinner table as soon as he could. He wanted to get back upstairs to his Airfix models, Tonka toys, and comics. He was a quiet, introspective little boy; small for his age and I worried about him. All the bloody time. Like every decent parent in the world, I'd fallen hopelessly in love with my child. I didn't want anything to hurt him, ever. Impossible, of course, but it didn't stop me wanting it.

Lizzie put the dishes in the centre of the table and I poured two glasses of white wine and some cherry Panda Pops for Thomas. Lizzie spooned lasagne onto our plates and handed me a couple of slices of garlic bread. She had cut some plain white bread with lashings of butter for Thomas. The lasagne was piping hot from the oven. Its topping of gooey cheese was still bubbling and the tomato sauce looked like edible molten lava.

I told Thomas to wait a minute or two. We blew on our plates together to cool the food down, pretending we were blowing out candles on a birthday cake.

Thomas started laughing wildly, wriggling around in his seat. The phone rang and Lizzie went to answer it.

'All right, son,' I said, 'time to settle down and eat your dinner.' He picked up a slice of bread in his small fingers and bit into, leaving a tiny smear of butter on his chin.

'It's for you,' Lizzie said. 'Andy, the trainee from school?'

'I wonder what he wants?' I couldn't think of any reason why Andy would be phoning.

'He says it's important.'

The hallway was always gloomy, even - or especially - when the evening sun threw a little bloodied light onto the pamment floor.

'Hi Andy what's up?'

But, of course, it wasn't Andy.

Billy must have copied the number down.
'I really need to see you. It's important. Please, Jack.'

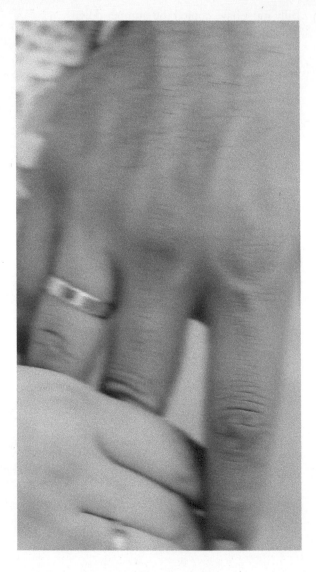

'Jesus Christ, Billy! You're crazy. I'm not going to leave my wife. Not now, not ever.'

chapter seven

'MEN BOUND OVER AFTER PINK GRAFFITI PROTEST'

Four gay men have been bound over to keep the peace for 18 months by City of London magistrates after painting pink triangles on the Fleet Street office of the Daily Star. The pink graffiti protest was provoked by a rising tide of anti-gay articles in the British tabloid press.

GAY TIMES, JUNE 1988

i

I said very little to Billy over the phone. I was afraid of being overhead. Now in the smothering dark with Lizzie sleeping next to me, I imagined all sorts of calamities: Syphilis? Hepatitis? AIDS? We'd been careful, we'd taken all the right precautions, but we'd also been very drunk. Had we slipped up somehow? What if I'd passed something on to Lizzie; she was the innocent in all this.

105

Murder of the Innocents. I told myself, stop. None of this was real. I'd find out soon enough. But still I hardly slept. It was a very long time before the night gave way to a watery dawn.

I shaved and dressed. The man staring back at me in the mirror was a strangely hollow man - one of the hollow men, oddly detached from his body, stuffed with straw.

I told Lizzie that Andy had left some important documents at school; he needed me to let him in so he could pick them up.

I promised Thomas I'd be back in time to take him for his tennis lesson.

Then I drove to Billy's flat in Stratford.

ii

Jack is stuck behind a delivery van for most of the way. Its rattling exhaust spews out palls of tarry smoke. Billy's building looks soviet in the sickly sunlight; an unloved block in a forgotten neighbourhood in Stalingrad. He gives Jack a colourless smile as he opens the door. The living room is more chaotic than Jack remembers it. A confusion of magazines, dirty cups and saucers, CDs piled precariously next to the stereo, discarded clothes thrown across the back of the sofa.

In contrast Billy looks very neat and tidy. He's wearing a gold hoop in each ear, and a neatly-pressed brown check shirt tucked into faded Levis. He looks like he's stepped out of a boy band poster. He looks good, Jack thinks. Christ, he looks great. Jack guesses it's all for his benefit. Billy Soanes knows what makes men tick. He is softening the blow he's about to let fall: looking so good, it'll be impossible to hate him when he delivers the terrible news.

He offers Jack coffee, his eyes searching the room, settling on two dirty mugs at the foot of an armchair. He picks them up. Jack tells him he doesn't want anything and Billy's expression is strained as he plunges his hands into his pockets.

Then, silence.

Jack breaks it. 'Don't call me at home again, Billy.'

'I had to see you, Jack. I didn't know what else to do.' Billy is fidgeting, as if with the unbearableness of what he is about to say.

'Just don't ever call me at home.'

Now the boy looks like a startled muntjac. Jack knows he needs to handle him carefully. He softens his tone. 'What is it you wanted to see me about?'

Billy closes his eyes, calling up the words he's obviously rehearsed a hundred times. 'I'm sorry about what happened, about how it all ended. I really screwed up.'

'It doesn't matter now.' Jack doesn't need any more of this. He holds his voice steady, keeps his patience.

'I want you to love me again, Jack. I can be the person you want me to be.'

'Good God, I thought you were going to tell me you had AIDS or something.' Jack almost wants to laugh; whether it's Billy's ludicrous naïvety or his own immense relief, he can't be sure.

'I love you,' Billy says, struggling under the weight of the confession.

'No you don't,' Jack says coolly. 'We fooled around for a

few days. It wasn't enough to fall in love.'

'It was enough for me.'

'Don't be silly. You're a great kid. You'll find someone who can give you what you want. That person just isn't me.'

'You know that's not true, Jack. You're saying it because you're afraid, but I can help you. I can give you strength.'

'To do what?'

'Leave your wife. Be with me.'

'Jesus Christ, Billy! You're crazy. I'm not going to leave my wife.'

'You love me. You don't love her. You told me you don't love her.'

'For God's sake, I was drunk. We were both drunk.'

'People don't lie about things like that. Specially when they're drunk.' He is backing Jack into a corner and Jack's instinct is to lash out.

'You and I had a fling,' Jack says. 'That's all. It's over.'

'It's not. It'll never be over. I love you. I live for you. And you love me. I know you do. I can see it in your face.' He is lost; a bewildered little boy.

Something deep inside Jack wants to hold him, comfort him, father him. But he tells himself - tries to convince himself - the boy isn't his problem. He can't be. The stakes are too high. If he lets Billy get to him, he'll lose everything. He's never been so cornered, so wrong-footed in his life.

'I know it's all my fault.' Billy is on the edge of tears. 'I've screwed it all up. Please can't we start again? I can put it right, I promise. It'll be different this time. I'll be perfect.'

'It's not about that. Aren't you listening to me? I have a

108

wife! A child! That's my life. Whether you like it or not, it's the life I've chosen. I've got to live with that choice.' Jack can hear his own voice rising. He stops, holds his hands out in a mollifying gesture. 'I can't give you what you want, Billy. Not now, not ever. You have to understand that.'

'I'll make you love me again, Jack. I'll make it right.'

What Billy is saying is too dangerous; Jack can't hold back any longer; he grabs the boy and shakes him, trying to get some sense into him, trying to make him see. 'I don't love you!' he says. Billy tries to put his arms around Jack's neck but Jack pushes him away.

'You *do* love me.' He's sobbing now in earnest, tears running down his cheeks, head shaking from side to side as if to deny an unpalatable truth.

'You have got to stop this, Billy. Don't call me again.' Jack starts for the door. The place is like an enclosure in an animal house - stifling and stinking.

Billy is clinging to him. 'Please don't go Jack. I can't bear it. I need you.'

'No!' Jack shouts. He tears Billy off him. He has to show Billy he is unbreachable or the boy could ruin him. Like an alpha male in a troop of baboons, he attacks Billy, pinning him against the wall. 'You don't know me Billy! You can't love me. It's childish, a childish infatuation.' With each sentence, he pushes him against the wall.

Then he relaxes his grip, sickened by the realisation of what he's doing, by who he's become. He doesn't want to be this man. Billy pushes back against him, sobbing fitfully.

'It's not true. Stop lying, you bastard! You can't do this. I'll tell your wife, Jack. You fucking hypocrite!'

Jack takes hold of the boy's collar, pulling him closer until they're eyeball to eyeball in a strange intimacy of violence.

'Don't you dare threaten me! This is over.' He lets go and Billy slides down the wall like a broken doll.

Jack has to get out of there. He's suffocating, nauseated.

iii

I stormed down the hallway, pursued by Billy's whining. This thing with Billy seemed like it was never going to end. I hurried down into the street. I drove aimlessly. I needed time to calm down.

I parked up and struck out over Westward Hatch common. I shouldn't have manhandled Billy but I didn't know how else to put a stop to it. I couldn't let him tear my family apart. I cursed him silently. I cursed the whole damned fucked-up world. I cursed the rotten, twisted god that had made me like this. I sat on a bench opposite Churchill's statue. I was Judas - I'd betrayed my wife, my son, even Billy, and yet the person I'd betrayed most was myself. I was playing a sly game with other people's lives. I straightened up and took a couple of deep breaths. I wished I'd never gone to that gay bar. I wished I'd never met Billy Soanes. I wished I'd never got married. I wished I'd never been born. I wished I were dead and gone. *You will be taken to a place of execution and hanged by the neck until you are dead.*

Then I thought of Thomas. Fatherless. I checked the

110

black and gold Casio on my wrist, another present from Lizzie. I'd promised Thomas I would be back in good time. I needed to put Billy out of my mind. I needed to get it together.

iv

Thomas rushed out to meet me and bounced around like an excited bunny as we loaded our tennis gear into the car. His uncomplicated joy was the counteragent I needed. I was so glad to be spending the afternoon with him; he was untainted by the frailty or the cruelty of the adult world. I wished he could stay like that forever.

I booked one of the practice courts and hired a tennis ball launcher so we could try out his forehand grip and swing. I showed him the neutral stance: feet, hips and shoulders sideways; bodyweight on the front leg; heel of the back foot raised. I knew he was still too young to take it all in. After a few minutes of missing the shot and pulling faces like the world was going to end, he got the hang of the stroke and started connecting with the ball - hitting it mostly into the net. I wasn't entirely sure he liked tennis, even though he said he did. Maybe he just wanted to please daddy.

Afterwards, I took him for a cheeseburger and fries, and a super-sized milkshake. He could only manage half the milkshake and I finished it off for him.

v

It was more than a week since I'd seen Billy and he hadn't called the house again. Like summer turning to autumn, or the waning of the moon, my life was moving into its next safe and predictable phase. I had returned to my reassuring, precious little lie. I knew I'd go back to another seedy bar eventually, pick up another boy; it was something I couldn't stop but I'd never fly so close to the flame again. I hoped Billy was okay. He deserved something better, someone better than me.

I fixed a date to help Nigel plant his rhododendrons. Sandie was aching to try out (or show off) her new fondue set so she suggested I bring Lizzie along and we make an evening of it. We dropped Thomas at my mother's. Lizzie, as usual, was the designated driver.

Nigel chose a shady spot in the corner of the garden. I did most of the hard graft, digging a large wide hole, making sure it wasn't too deep to drown the root ball. Nigel had bought some lovely mature plants and they had to be moved using a large barrow. Lizzie hovered fretfully as we lowered them into the earth. She didn't want back problems interrupting our sex life again.

Once the plants were in the ground, I saturated them with water and added copious quantities of mulch. Then Nigel and I sat out on the patio with a couple of beers while Lizzie and Sandie got dinner ready in the kitchen.

Safe.

The air was lifeless, no breeze to stir the branches, no comforting rustle of leaves. Calm before the storm? My tee shirt clung to me, sticky with sweat.

'Are you all set for going away?' I asked Nigel.

'I've just got to pick up some dollars and travellers

112

cheques. Then we're all ready for ten days of glorious Florida sunshine.'

'Enjoy it. You lucky bastard.' We clinked bottlenecks.

'Not too late to book a little get away yourselves.'

'No,' I told him. 'We need to get the extension done in the autumn, so we're watching the pennies.'

'Just stick it all on the never-never, old chum.'

'There's too much on the never-never already,' I said, 'and Thomas's school fees seem to go up every term.'

Nigel sighed. 'C'est la vie.'

Safe.

'Dinner's ready, boys,' Sandie called from the kitchen.

'I'm bloody ravenous,' Nigel said.

'I don't know why.' I slapped him on the back. 'I did all the work.'

'Bugger off. I did my bit.'

Nigel uncorked a bottle of Beaujolais and filled our glasses. Sandie brought a large pot of creamy melted cheese fondue to the table and set it down carefully next to a basket of crusty French loaves.

'Looking forward to your holiday?' I asked her.

'Yes,' she said a little hesitantly. 'I still can't get used to not having the boys with us, though.' (Both their sons were backpacking across Europe.)

'It'll be bloody marvellous,' Nigel laughed.

Sandie didn't look as happy at the prospect of a holiday with just her husband for company. She'd already told me she was worried about the boys travelling on their own.

'Is your NQT all set now?' she said as she tore off a piece of bread and dipped it in the pot.

'All fine,' I said.

Safe.

'He seems very keen,' Lizzie said. 'Jack had to go and open up the school for him last week.'

'Really? What an earth for?'

'He'd left some stuff behind,' I said. 'Some bits and pieces he needed for lesson planning. It was no big deal.'

'God,' said Sandie, 'he is an eager beaver. Just the kind of man we need at Roughton Road.'

'I think he'll do well,' I said.

All the time I could feel Nigel's eyes on me.

vi

'Come on, handsome,' Lizzie said softly, 'we've got a child to pick up and a church jumble sale to get to.' Last night was a bit hazy. Nigel had forced a couple of large brandies down me at the end of the evening. My head felt as battered as a football at the final whistle. Lizzie was already showered and dressed, and raring to go.

My mother lived five minutes' walk from Snaresbrook station. She was an early riser, even at the weekends. She'd have me up and out of the house first thing every Saturday. Then we'd head over to Dalston to visit my grandmother. Her meagre council flat had that smell of scrubbed decay - Palmolive soap and old lino. The afternoon would be spent ambling through the crowds at Walthamstow market, buying the week's groceries.

114

Thomas's eager face appeared at the window as soon as we pulled up outside my mother's well-kept 1930s semi. He was washed and brushed, clutching his overnight bag like a shield. He looked so small with his little denim jacket buttoned right up to the chin. I undid the top few buttons and gave him an enormous hug.

'Did you have a good time?'

'It was okay.'

Lizzie and I exchanged looks; my mother's idea of appropriate, organised fun didn't always go down too well. After my father's death, she'd become very driven. She had something to prove to the world - that she could cope alone; that she could single-handedly guide her only son on the path to success; make of me a respectable husband and father. She was delighted when I went into teaching. Now she was turning her ambitions towards Thomas. But he wasn't ready just yet to fight his way to the top. I wasn't convinced he ever would be. Often he just wanted to sit quietly, lost in his own world of comics and model planes.

The Memorial Hall was already buzzing with eager volunteers. Eileen Dobkins, no-nonsense chair of the social committee, strode towards us, staring imperiously through wire-rimmed spectacles. Thomas hooked his arm through mine and looked at her uncertainly, chewing his nails.

'Aaah! Jack Huntley,' she thundered. 'Just the man!' She waved her clipboard towards a stack of grey plastic trestle tables. 'All these need putting out, my love. Roger will help you.' Roger Dobkins - fourteen-ish; freckles; Def Leppard tee shirt and resentful look - skulked along behind his mother.

'Jack's injured his back,' Lizzie told her.

'They're very light, dear,' Eileen bristled, 'my cat could carry them.'

'It's not a problem,' I said.

Lizzie rolled her eyes at me and took Thomas by the hand as Eileen ushered them towards the refreshments stall.

Roger helped me set out the tables at regular intervals in the middle of the hall and along the sides. The hall had a raised platform at one end and the whole room was starkly lit, as if for an interrogation. By the time we were finished, Lizzie and Thomas had filled the tea and coffee canisters, stacked paper plates, arranged plastic cutlery and napkins, and Lizzie was busy pricing up muffins, cakes and sandwiches. The temptation was proving too much for my son who'd left a greasy finger mark on some of the iced buns. Not unexpectedly, Lizzie screamed at him, and the entire hall went suddenly quiet. I took him over to the entrance and told him he could help me with the tickets and cash box as people came in.

'Do we have to stay here all day, daddy?'

'No, darling. Someone else takes over at midday and then we'll go and, on our way out, I'll buy you a slice of cake to have at home.' I winked at him.

'Is mummy coming with us?'

'No, mummy's here till four.' Still wary after Lizzie's outburst, he seemed quite pleased to hear that.

vii

There were two letters on the mat when we got home: my monthly Barclaycard statement and an envelope

116

addressed to me in a spidery script. I poured out a Pepsi for Thomas and put his slice of Victoria sponge on a plate, then I retreated to my study with the mail. I knew who the letter was from before I opened the envelope. A handful of glossy photographs fell out. They were all of me in bed, the covers thrown off in the heat of the late summer morning. There were five photos in all and in every one I was naked. Billy must have photographed me while I slept. My mouth went dry as I read what Billy had written.

My darling Jack,

Please forgive me for what happened last time we were together. I've missed you so much. I can't stop thinking about you. And about us.

I don't know why I took these pictures. I guess I wanted to have something of you close to me even when we were apart. I've slept with them by my bed, looked at them for hours and ached for you.

I know how much you must be hurting. But you can't go on living a lie, pretending you love your wife. You're poisoning yourself and wasting your life. You have to understand that.

I know you don't think we can be together, but you're wrong. We can make it work. You need me just as much as I need you.

I love you so much Jack. Tell Lizzie you don't want her. Tell her you can't play along with the charade anymore. Be with me. The one you really love. I know you and me are meant to be. You know it too, don't you?

I love you my darling.

Billy.

I flinched as the door to my study opened and Thomas looked in at me excitedly. 'Daddy, will you play snakes and ladders with me now?'

I thought of Tony and of Billy, and I cupped one of Lizzie's breasts, savouring its softness as I licked her nipple.

chapter eight

Jack meets Billy at the foot of Centre Point. Its thirty-four storeys cast an impossibly long shadow over London's busiest street. It's a sombre and strangely cheerless place despite the nearby bustle of shoppers and buskers. As a drunken teen, Jack had stood with his back to the building and looked up. The concrete facade rose into the cold black sky behind him, giving him a feeling of falling or hurtling headlong into oblivion. No one can find you out or accuse you in oblivion. No one can make you pay in oblivion. Now he wishes he could rise into the sky and disappear, a dust mote exiled on the sighing wind.

Billy is standing awkwardly in a black bomber jacket and *Choose Life* tee shirt as Jack approaches. He says they should go to the First Out coffee shop and they walk the short distance without saying a word to each other.

The handsome black guy behind the counter catches their mood and his smile fades as he jots down their order.

They sit at a table underneath an out-of-date poster for June's Lesbian Strength March. They sit as far away from other people as they can get in the small, whitewashed space.

'Why did you send me the letter?' Jack asks simply.

'I didn't know what else to do. You told me not to phone you.'

'I told you not to contact me. This can't go on, Billy. I don't know what it is you're expecting from me.'

'I can see you're unhappy, Jack.' He reaches for Jack's hand and Jack pulls it away.

'Too right I'm unhappy. What if my wife had seen the letter? And those pictures. Jesus Christ!'

'Don't be angry with me. It's because I love you. Can't you see that?'

'No, I can't!' Jack lowers his voice. 'Whatever you think is going on… isn't. There's nothing between us. You have to accept that.'

'It's not true.' Billy leans forward. 'I can see that you're scared, but don't be. It'll be tough when you leave Lizzie but I'll be there for you every step of the way. You have to believe me. I'd do anything for you, Jack. I'd die for you, Jack.'

'For crying out loud,' Jack snaps now. 'I don't want any of this Billy. I don't want to be with you.'

'You told me you loved me. In your house. In your bed.'

'I was drunk. I probably said a lot of things.'

The server approaches the table, puts two cappuccinos between them and retreats quickly. 'I don't want you to contact me again, Billy. No phone calls. No letters. No photos. Nothing. Ever. Do you understand?'

'Stop shutting me out, Jack.'

'Move on with your life. Find somebody else. Leave me alone.'

'You don't mean that.'

'Yes I do. I do mean it. I don't know how many different ways I can say it.'

'I love you Jack.'

Jack looks at the boy uneasily. '*I don't love you Billy.*'

The light dies in Billy's eyes. Jack doesn't want to hurt him any more but he doesn't know what else to do.

'You said you don't love your wife,' Billy mutters. 'Then you made love to me.'

'I'm sorry I said what I said. I didn't love you then and I don't love you now. I will never love you. We had sex a few times. That's all.'

'It's not true.' Billy's voice dies away. 'Why are you being like this?'

'You have to give up on this fantasy. We aren't a couple.'

'Neither are you and your wife. Not really.'

'But we are. We are a proper married couple. Man and wife. And we do love each other.'

'Stop lying!' Billy chokes on the words. He's going to cry again.

'I'm going now Billy,' Jack says quietly. 'I don't hold anything against you. I really don't. But you've got to stop all this. I don't want to see you any more.'

'But I love you.' Billy's face is wet. The other customers study their plates awkwardly, or the walls, or each other's faces. Jack stands up.

'Please Jack!'

Jack opens his wallet and tosses a couple of pound coins onto the table. Then he walks quickly out of the cafe.

I put the bucket of balls beside me on the baseline. Keeping my grip relaxed, I let my thumb and index finger form a perfect 'v' along the handle of the racquet. I tossed the ball into the air, brought the racquet up behind me to 'scratch my back' with the head and in one fluid movement swung the racquet forwards, connecting with the ball at the highest point. The ball spun through the air and bounced neatly in the centre of the service box before twisting away across the court. I hit another, and another, finding my mark each time. Practising my game was a way of releasing the tension. Concentrating on nothing but my serve helped me forget everything else.

The next ball slammed into the net and I cursed, and dropped to the floor for ten push-ups - my self-imposed penalty each time I missed my mark.

'You go tiger!' I looked up to see my coach, Hakesh, walking towards me. 'I didn't know you were coming in today.'

'I wasn't planning to,' I told him, 'but I had a little spare time.' Hakesh nodded, his eyes were the deepest hazel, his coal-black hair slicked neatly back; it never seemed to ruffle even after a five-set match. In the showers his body was lean and wiry, he was uncut, long and dark. His father owned a textile company in Debden and Hakesh was the one son who didn't want to go into the business. His family's wealth meant he didn't really need the money and playing tennis all day was the dream come true. Hence he was always in good spirits - wide and casual grin, smiling eyes. He was also an inveterate flirt.

'How's that lovely wife of yours?'

'She's fine.'

124

'Still gorgeous?'

'Oh, yes.'

'You are one lucky son-of-a-bitch, mate.'

'Don't I know it.'

Hakesh had met Lizzie last summer at a charity dinner at the club. She'd worn a clinging black cocktail dress and his roaming gaze fixed on her early in the evening. Ever since, he never failed to enquire after her good health and general deliciousness.

'Sure we can't tempt her to a few lessons?'

'You wish.'

'I've got ten minutes before my next lesson,' he said purposefully. 'How about we practise a few rallies?'

His serve was faster and more powerful than mine. He hit the ball deep, forcing me back to the baseline, left and right, and racing to the middle for the return shot. He wore me out in no time.

'Time's up, mate. I've got a stunning divorcee waiting for me on court five.'

'Lucky boy. Thanks for the free torture session.' I rolled my eyes. We shook hands and he trotted away. My legs were aching and I flopped down at the side of the court to rest before going back to my serve. I wiped my forehead with my sweat band. Billy Soanes was still in there, working away at the back of my mind.

iii

Thomas stared intently at the screen as he munched on his popcorn and licked his sticky fingers, lost in the world of Castle Grayskull. Skeletor made his entrance, striding down the great hall, black-clad storm troopers on either side. He turned his black cowl to the camera, revealing his ghoulish skull face. His voice boomed, his message violent and murderous. Thomas jerked his head away, hiding his face in my side. I remembered how terrified I felt as a boy watching the witches attack the ship in *Jack the Giant Killer*. Everything was so real to my young mind. I squeezed him gently. 'It's okay,' I whispered. 'It's just a man in a mask. It's only pretend.'

We put Thomas to bed early that night. While Lizzie got him into his pyjamas and read him a story, I opened a bottle of Rioja and flicked through the television channels. The glug-glugging of the wine was a homely sound, a totem of a normal, middle-class family life.

Safe.

Lizzie rested her head against my chest and I wrapped her in my arms. Here was the even-keeled life I had to stick to. The only film we could find was a workaday mystery about a playwright trying to unmask a murderer. We must have nodded off. I had no idea how long we'd been asleep.

I stroked Lizzie's face and she sat up sleepily. I kissed her. She took our glasses in her hands and I followed her upstairs with the bottle.

I was pulling off her clothes. We drank more wine. It was heady and impulsive and we were tumbling into bed together and I thought of Tony and of Billy, and I cupped one of Lizzie's breasts, savouring its softness as I licked her nipple.

Tony's nipple. Tony's skin.

Her fingers were round my shaft, moving up and down in gentle practised movements. 'Harder,' I told her as I pushed her down towards the tip of my cock and her lips took me in.

Billy's lips, Billy's fingers.

I thrust harder. And she gagged.

Billy. Thrusting into Billy.

She was gripping my butt and her nails were digging into my skin and I thrust harder and rougher.

But now I was aware of something else. There it was again. Across the hall. A whimper: Thomas.

I reached for my pyjama bottoms.

'Skeletor,' he said, 'he's in here!'

'It's all right, chicken. It was just a bad dream. It's all okay. Daddy's here now.' I held him tight and kissed the top of his head.

'Daddy, I'm frightened.' His lip was shiny and trembling. He was tired and small and overcome by terror. Lizzie appeared, tying up her dressing gown and took him from me.

'I think this little tinker had better sleep in mummy's bed tonight?' I said, winking at her. She looked at me ruefully. 'I'll make it up to you,' I mouthed as she walked away, our son staring back at me.

I got into bed in the spare room and turned off the light.

Billy.

127

I wondered where he'd gone, what he'd done after I'd left him in the cafe.

I'd smashed serves on a tennis court to forget him. I'd worked for hours, good back-breaking work in the garden.

Billy.

I felt the heat rising. I wanted to throw him down and plunge into him. I wanted to fuck him till sunlight crept in through the open window.

Billy.

His crazy fantasies about us. His temper. The odd blue eyes. Slowly I slid my hand down beneath the sheets, down over my belly, down under the waistband of my pyjamas.

iv

Thomas was prodding my chest. 'Mummy says you're a lazy boy.'

'Oh I am, am I?' I lifted him up and tickled him then pulled up his tee shirt and blew a huge raspberry on his tummy. He giggled and writhed and gasped for breath. I sat him on the bed next to me and he curled his small arms around me. The house was warm and there was the smoky tang of bacon frying. 'I suppose daddy had better get up then, hadn't he?' I said.

Lizzie handed me a plate of bacon and eggs. She was wearing a simple shift dress that suited her very much. She was beautiful. She leaned into me and there was the mix of Lizzie and the honey-and-musk of Dior Poison. A thunderstorm had swaggered in during the early hours. The air in the room had a remote freshness to it and

128

Lizzie's skin was a little cold to the touch.

'Thomas,' I said, 'run up and get mummy's cardigan for her.' I heard him bounding up the stairs. His footsteps banged across the bedroom floor, making the light overhead rattle.

Lizzie called up to him from the doorway not to run in the house.

I poured hot milk into the coffee and filled Thomas's glass with orange juice. Lizzie kissed me as I placed the glass on the table.

'I hope we're going to pick up where we left off last night, handsome.'

'Definitely.'

She pulled me to her and her tongue was inside my mouth, and I caressed the small of her back. She stopped, resting her hands on my chest and looked at me quizzically. I knew what she was thinking, it was that telepathic connection between couples who have been together for a long time. 'What's taking him so long?' I said.

'Maybe, he can't find it,' she said. She kissed my hand, taking two of my fingers in her mouth, sucking them slowly. I pulled her roughly to me, tasting her again. She giggled, surrendering to the moment. I kissed her and kissed her. Life was back to normal again. Our life. Our kitchen. Our house. Our family.

Then there was a heavy thud from the floor above and Thomas started screaming.

'It's sometimes, but not always, used during anal intercourse. It's also known as poppers.'

chapter nine

i

I held Thomas in my arms. His face was scarlet. His breathing stuttered out in little gasps. Lizzie was whispering, *'Oh my God, oh my God, oh my God...'* And now I was running down the staircase and Thomas's head was lolling against my chest and I yelled at Lizzie to get the car keys. *'Oh my God, oh my God, oh my God...'* Thomas had passed out.

Now I was driving fast, driving too fast and Lizzie was in the back seat with Thomas, stroking his hair, and his breathing was very shallow: *husk, huk, husk, huk* and the road was against us, a hideous obstacle course of pedestrians on crossings and slow-moving lorries and buses and Sunday drivers on a weekday morning and I was panicking, and terrified that my only child was going to die. I breaknecked past the *Accident and Emergency* sign and pulled up too sharply, hitting a concrete bollard, and took Thomas from Lizzie; and now we were running towards the hospital, running into two ambulance men coming the other way who switched instantly and oh-so-beautifully to smooth and well-practised procedure, and took our little boy from us and lifted him onto a stretcher, and took him swiftly into the hospital as we followed, and doors swung shut behind them and we were left to wait and imagine and dread.

Next a nurse appeared and fired a volley of questions at us:

How old is Thomas?
Is he an epileptic?
Is he taking any medication?
Has he been abroad in the past few weeks?

I heard my own voice in answer as if coming from a long way off. Lizzie just stared at the nurse. And the questions kept on coming:

Does he use an inhaler?
Does he have any chronic conditions or allergies?
Any history of fitting?

And the nurse told us, briskly but kindly enough, to wait and went back inside.

Thomas was gone, spirited away to another part of the hospital and we were alone in the kind of hell-born nightmare every parent dreads. I put my arm around Lizzie.

'Whatever's wrong with him?' she said.

'I don't know.'

'Tell me he's not going to die, Jack.'

'The doctors will look after him. He's in the best place now.' I sounded as reassuring as I could. 'They'll know what to do. He's not going to die. I promise.' She took a deep breath and sobbed. 'I'll get you some water,' I said.

And the receptionist nodded towards a drinks dispenser and I got two bottles of water and two cans of coke. Lizzie barely acknowledged me as I handed her the water. She put the bottle on the floor at her feet and then I took her hand in mine and we sat in silence. Our little family bubble, our sanctuary of routines and jokes and funny asides had been shattered by something we didn't understand. A father should be able to protect his child from danger; foresee the threat and neutralise it. I had failed. I began a silent, painful postmortem: was I right to drive Thomas to the hospital? Should I have called an ambulance? Had I done more harm than good?

'Mr and Mrs Huntley?' The doctor was standing in front of us and we stood up like children in front of the school principal. 'I'm Doctor Rickman,' he said and I didn't know whether to shake his hand or not. 'Can you tell me what your son was doing before he collapsed?' he asked.

'He was upstairs looking for my cardigan,' Lizzie said. 'Is he going to be all right?'

'Yes,' the doctor frowned slightly, 'but I'd like to keep him in.' And he cleared his throat and continued, 'It's standard procedure, particularly for an incident of this nature involving a child.'

'But what's wrong with him?' I said.

The doctor frowned again. 'He seems to have inhaled a substance. There's burning to the skin around his nostrils and also on his fingers and, judging from those symptoms, the substance looks to be amyl nitrate.'

'What's that?' Lizzie said.

The doctor looked uncomfortable. 'It's a type of narcotic.'

'A narcotic?'

'To put it plainly, Mrs Huntley, it's a recreational drug. It's sometimes, but not always, used during anal intercourse. It's also known as poppers.' He shifted his weight. 'It's often used, but again not exclusively, by homosexuals.'

And my stomach turned over and my mouth was full of cotton wool.

And 'I don't understand,' said Lizzie.

'We'll be running some tests,' said the doctor, 'but I think we'll find amyl nitrate is the culprit.'

'But our son is going to be okay?' I said and my voice was small, a shadow-voice, almost a whisper.

'Yes, he'll recover. But we'd like to keep him in for tonight. Just to be on the safe side.' He paused. 'Your personal lives are your own business, of course. But do keep these kinds of substances locked away in future.'

And I couldn't look at Lizzie as we followed the doctor to the children's ward.

The room was starkly functional, only a small effort had been made to brighten it. A peeling mural of some well-known cartoon characters ran along one wall: Bugs Bunny chewing on a carrot, Wile E. Coyote doggedly pursuing the Road Runner. At the far end was a small play area with low, brightly coloured tables and chairs, and a pile of soft toys and board games scattered around, and a beleaguered student nurse directing some children to tidy it all up. From what I could tell, the patients ranged from infants to top juniors, and some were with their parents, and others were amusing themselves or playing in small groups.

Doctor Rickman pulled the curtains across to give us some privacy and told us to keep it short. Thomas looked tiny, swallowed up by the stark hospital bedclothes. He was shaking as I kissed him; and I was the cause of this, that particular darkness inside me. *Billy.* Billy's bottle of poppers. *Me inside Billy.* Despite all my careful searching, I'd overlooked it, and it was Thomas who was paying the price. I hated myself for everything that I was.

ii

There it was underneath our bed: a little brown bottle lying on its side, the screw-top a few inches away. I took it downstairs to throw it in the bin but Lizzie snatched it from me. 'Where the hell did this come from, Jack?' I didn't know what to say. 'I'm asking you a question, damn you!' Lizzie waved the evidence in front of me. 'You've had somebody here. Who was she?' She threw the bottle at me and it clattered onto the floor.

'It's mine,' I told her, my voice catching. 'I got it from a bloke at the club. It releases adrenaline, gives you a rush. I thought it would make me quicker, faster. Play better.'

Another lie in the great long list of lies, a dynasty of lies.

'So you're taking drugs now!' The colour rose in her cheeks. 'And our son is in the hospital. What kind of a man are you? I don't know you at all, Jack. What's got into you?'

'Nothing's got into me,' I said, still unable to meet her gaze. 'D'you think I wanted this to happen? I'm sorry. Okay?'

'No, it's not okay!' She threw her hands up. 'I don't understand you. You've been so strange lately. How long have you been taking this stuff?'

'Not long.'

'I don't believe you!' She charged past me, and I grabbed her arm.

'Lizzie, please.'

'Let go of me!' She twisted away. The door to the bathroom slammed.

Lizzie spent the night in the spare room. I stayed well away from her, sleeping downstairs on the sofa. Except I didn't sleep. My back ached. I stared at the light in the ceiling and the long loop of cord hanging down.

Lizzie finished her cereal in silence well before me. She telephoned the hospital then disappeared upstairs again. When I couldn't bear it any longer, I went to find her. She was lying on the bed with a book but I knew she hadn't read a word.

'I promise this won't happen again,' I said. 'Please forgive me. You know I'd never intentionally do anything to hurt Thomas. Please believe me.'

She glanced up at me briefly. 'We'd better get to the hospital,' she said as she brushed past me.

Lizzie's preferred form of retribution was silence. I knew the signs. It was like she was banishing me from her mind. It was like I didn't exist. Somewhere deep down, I wished I didn't.

Doctor Rickman had completed his rounds but we had to wait for a hospital porter to take Thomas in a wheelchair. That was the protocol, we were told.

It seemed an interminable wait.

The room was hot. There was little breeze from outside. Thomas was restless. Lizzie asked the staff nurse for the third time when she thought the porter might come. She was met with an offhand remark and a shrug. We encouraged Thomas to play with his new friend, a boy a little older than him, who was also due to go home but his parents, so far, were a no-show. Thomas managed one game of snakes and ladders. Then he was back on the bed, his face buried in the pillow. He'd never been in hospital before. He wanted the familiarity of home and his own toys.

In the end, I picked him up and carried him out to the car myself. It was my first step on a long road of reparations for the all the harm I'd done.

Lizzie fretted around Thomas as if he would break. I holed up in my study. There were always stacks of school papers to sort. Sorting papers was comfortingly practical and dull, and it gave me a little time and space to think.

I emerged after an hour to find Thomas dozing off on the sofa. I brought down his Bugs Bunny blanket and wrapped him in it. Lizzie looked up from her *Woman's Realm.*

'We should go away,' I said, 'just the two of us, like we used to when we first met.'

'What about Thomas?'

'Your parents could come and look after him. They love house-sitting for us. And he loves them. They'd take him on days out. He'd have a great time.'

'I don't know, Jack.'

'We don't have to go for too long,' I said. 'Just a few days.'

I was desperate. Everything seemed to be slipping through my fingers.

I took her hand. 'We both need a holiday, baby. A proper break from everything. And I need you. I need you so much.'

I could feel her beginning to weaken. 'Please Lizzie.' She knew, just as I did, that things hadn't been right for a while. We'd spent so much time building my career, smartening up our home, nurturing our son. We'd forgotten to nurture each other.

'I'm not sure.' She was holding out on me. 'What if something else happens and we're on the other side of the world?'

'It won't, and we don't have to go that far.'

'You don't have any more nasty surprises up your sleeve?' She half-laughed. The knife was in and I knew I deserved it. 'I just don't feel comfortable leaving Thomas right now.'

'I know,' I said. 'It could be just a short hop. Remember the cottage on the cliffs at Highcliff, the one we stayed in when you were pregnant, with the balcony overlooking the sea?'

138

We used to sit out in the evenings and look across the water and it was one of the times we were happiest, before life got the better of us. No mortgage, no loans, no school runs.

'Yes,' she said. 'Yes, I do remember.'

I put a match to Billy's letter.

chapter ten

i

The evening sky was opalescent now, the sea a correspondingly pale and shimmering blue-green. Lizzie and I strolled hand-in-hand along the clifftops towards Pear Tree Cottage. In the distance, All Saints Church stood islanded in its little graveyard, as if standing watch over the shifting waters. Lizzie had left a chicken roasting in the oven and now the cottage was filled with the rich, warm aroma of the roast. I'd forgotten the wine and had to run back to the car at the cliff edge. The sea was very beautiful and it was still warm. We decided to eat on the balcony looking out over the sea. The waves fell in soft folds onto the sand. Our plates were piled high with slices of tender roast chicken, plenty of golden potatoes, carrots and peas and the whole lot drizzled over with steaming gravy.

'I always look forward to your roasts,' I said, 'and this is one of your best.'

Lizzie smiled faintly.

'Are we all set for the big day?' I said.

'The what?'

'Our wedding anniversary.'

'Sorry, I was miles away.'

I'd been working so hard to rekindle the intimacy between Lizzie and me. I had a dozen red roses delivered on the day we arrived. We'd taken long walks in Sheringham Park and Roman Camp, had a romantic dinner at the Blakeney Hotel, and sunbathed at Salthouse and beyond the revetments at Highcliff beach. We'd done so much lovemaking I thought my dick was going to drop off. I was determined to make things right between us; there was just too much at stake.

'You seem like you don't want a big party anymore,' I said. 'Would you rather just keep it low key?'

'No. It's our tenth anniversary,' said Lizzie. 'We should celebrate it. And all the invites have gone out now.'

For a while neither of us spoke. Then I said, 'I'm sorry about everything. I hope spending some time together like this, just the two of us… I hope I've been able to show you how much I love you.'

'Jack,' she said, setting down her glass of Rioja, 'you should have been more careful. Taking some kind of performance-enhancing drug, it's insane. Even if Thomas hadn't found it, it can't be good for you to be using like that.'

'I know. I wasn't thinking straight.'

'I still don't understand why you did it. It's not like you play for a living.'

'I always did want to be top dog.'

She looked at me like she didn't really believe me. I

wondered if she was still holding on to the idea that I'd been with another woman.

After what seemed like forever, she put her plate down and stood up and started massaging my shoulders. 'Why don't we just start again?' she said, bending down to kiss me. 'Why don't we go into the bedroom and you can show me how much of a top dog you really are.'

We drank and fucked into the early hours. It was our last night before returning to the real world of responsibility, and obligation.

For a brief moment, we were reliving a fiction that neither of us really believed in any more.

Pear Tree Cottage had been ours for three days and now it was over. But our relationship seemed to be on the road to recovery. I loaded up the car while Lizzie checked we hadn't left anything behind.

We drove back through Norfolk's and then Suffolk's farmlands, flattish and low-slung under huge skies, and we opened the windows against the mounting heat as the cassette player blasted out *Hounds of Love*, *Meat is Murder*, and *Dead Letter Office*. I didn't want the journey to end. At least the motorway took us straight to the northern edge of Westward Hatch and we didn't have to stop-start through London's baking centre.

Lizzie's parents were no gardeners and I returned to find the borders gasping for water in the hot afternoon sun. My father-in-law, Roy, that giant oak of a man with the telltale complexion of the enthusiastic drinker - I could talk - came purposefully towards me as I was watering the camellias.

'How's it going, Jack? Lizzie says you both had a nice time away.'

'It was good. The weather was nice. We even saw some live bands at the Highcliff Pavilion.'

'You youngsters and your music. It all sounds the same to me. The boys look like girls. Dear oh dear.' He was trying to sound jovial but there was something else under the jokey tone. He scratched the back of his neck. 'Listen, Jack. Have you got a minute?'

'Sure.' I switched off the hose and turned to face him. He was much bigger than me in all directions.

'Sally and I are just a bit concerned about what happened with Thomas. How could you leave paint stripper lying around like that?'

(The official story.)

'I was hurrying to finish up the decorating. It just slipped my mind. It won't happen again.'

He let out a laboured sigh. 'I don't know how to say this, so I'll just come right out with it. Is everything all right between you and my daughter?'

'It's been a difficult year at work but everything's fine. And with the renovations on the house, you know…?'

'If you're a bit short, we can help out.'

'That's very generous of you, Roy, but we're fine. We just needed a break - some time just to ourselves. Thanks for looking after Thomas for us.'

'You know we love seeing him. Just look after my grandson properly and treat my daughter right.' He was smiling but there was a tightness in his voice that suggested a warning. Or a threat. Roy was the archetypal 'man's man'. He owned a paper mill in Matlock Bath. He was a man of industry. I knew I was a tad too soft for him,

144

working in a 'namby-pamby' job. Men taught in secondary schools to keep the teenage lads in order. Infants and juniors were the domain of women - all poster paints and sewing kits; not serious; a queer career choice for a bloke.

ii

The small antique table was dotted with rust and some of the paint was peeling after one summer downpour too many. Lizzie and I had picked it up last year in Camden Passage. One of these days I'd get round to restoring it.

Paperwork didn't seem so bad in the garden in the summertime. I was looking over topic webs and lesson plans for the start of the new term, a mug of tea at my elbow. Eddie appeared at the garden gate, rifling through his postbag. He ambled across the lawn in baggy blue summer shorts, a shark's tooth earring dangling from one ear. He always looked to me like a dead ringer for Ian McCulloch.

'There you go, boss,' he said, handing me a wad of letters with a sunny smile.

'More junk mail?' I said, smiling in return.

'Nobody loves you, eh?'

I sorted through the bundle - bills, advertisements, a new Access card. Then, right at the bottom, a letter addressed to Lizzie. The uneven scrawl was unmistakable. Now I could hear Lizzie calling out and a moment later she appeared. She was taking Thomas to get a new school uniform; the prospect always made him muted and pouty. I stuffed Billy's letter under my stack of papers.

'We're off darling,' she said, kissing me on the top of

the head. 'Won't be back till this afternoon. We're going to meet aunty Sandie for lunch, aren't we?' She squeezed Thomas's hand. He was already muted. Already pouty.

'Won't she be jet lagged? They only got back yesterday.'

'Apparently not. You know Sandie. I've left a ham sandwich in the fridge.' Lizzie glanced at the pile of letters. 'Anything for me?'

'No,' I said, keeping my expression as even as possible. 'Nothing today.'

I watched her usher Thomas into the house and close the back door behind them. Then I heard the car rumble into life; tyres chewing the gravel.

I pulled out Billy's letter. I sat for a long time, staring at the envelope, willing it to be from someone else.

Then I tore it open.

Dear Lizzie,

I know this is going to hurt you and for that I'm deeply sorry but there's no good in hiding the truth from you. Your husband Jack is gay. He and I are lovers. While you were away, he brought me to your house and we made love in your bed. We spent wonderful days and nights together. During that time Jack was truly happy.

The truth is he doesn't love you. He has never loved you. He married you because he felt that it was the right thing to do. I know this is painful for you to hear but you have to let him go. He wants to be with me but he is torn between the life he really wants and his misguided feelings of loyalty to you.

I know you'll find someone else in time, someone who can

146

give you the love you truly deserve. That person isn't Jack. He loves me and I love him. We adore each other.

Please, Lizzie, I'm begging you. Let Jack go. Set him free. For both your sakes.

I'm so sorry that you had to find out this way. I understand how difficult it must be. But I wish you every happiness in the future.

With kindness,
Billy Soanes

I put a match to Billy's letter. I watched the flames eating through Billy's childish handwriting. The paper, and every deranged word on it, turned black and curled smokily into the air. This letter was gone. But he could send another one, then another, then another. My anger made me lightheaded. I hated Billy. I wanted to hurt Billy. I wanted to wipe Billy out.

The journey to Billy's flat was a blur.

The block of flats was more dilapidated than ever in the dry heat of August. I jabbed the intercom and a tinny voice spoke some words I couldn't make out.

'Let me in, Billy!' I barked into the speaker.

iii

Now Jack is at Billy's door. The door is open slightly. Jack smacks it aside and the door slams into the plaster,

147

and plaster falls. Billy stands at the end of the hallway. Jack storms towards him. Billy puts his hands up over his face. Jack clamps his fist around the neck of the boy's tee shirt. Jack snarls, 'You crazy freak!'

'Jack...' is all Billy manages to get out.

'You don't get it, do you?'

Jack is only anger now. Jack's hands are around Billy's throat. Jack is shaking Billy. Billy's head is rocking dangerously, stressing the delicate structure of his neck.

'I don't want you in my life! Stay out of my fucking life, Billy!'

Billy's knee rises in self-defence into Jack's crotch. The pain is like a sword running up deep inside. Jack doubles over. Jack curls up to protect himself. Jack pivots sideways to avoid a second blow.

Billy's mouth is moving but no sound is coming out. The veins are standing out on Billy's neck. And then Billy speaks. 'Get away from me, you bastard! You fucking heartless bastard! I hate you!'

The knife is bright in Billy's hands. The blade bites the skin of Jack's arm.

Jack jabs at Billy's solar plexus. Jack slams the air out of Billy.

Billy falls to his knees.

Blood runs down Jack's arm. Blood runs onto the floor.

'Don't you ever come near me or my family again. So help me.'

Billy is not looking at Jack.

Jack doesn't know if Billy hears him. Now Jack has only one thought: he must leave before he loses it.

Jack must not kill Billy.

Jack slams the car into gear. Jack reverses rapidly along the narrow road. Jack spins the wheel and the car twists out onto the main road.

And Jack has no idea where to go next.

*Her mother is from Kingston, her father Nigerian,
so she knows and loves the cooking of both countries.*

chapter eleven

i

Jack recognises him instantly: narrow shoulders, sober nordic features. He pulls over and calls Conor's name. Conor stops abruptly. Jack can tell he's struggling to remember who he is. Then recognition sparks.

'You're the guy going out with Billy,' Conor says. He sees Jack's bloodied arm. 'Jesus Christ! What happened?'

'It's a long story. Can we talk?'

'I was just going back to the flat,' Conor says.

Jack is afraid for him. 'I don't think that's a good idea. Billy and I just had a huge bust-up. Can I buy you a coffee? I really need to talk to someone.'

Conor gets into the car. 'Did Billy do this?'

Billy.

'Yes,' Jack says, 'but it's not all his fault. We had a really big fight. I went for him and he lashed out at me.'

'Let me drive. Let's get your arm sorted out.'

Conor doesn't live with Billy anymore. He's moved a few streets away to a dismal little pebble-dashed terrace. He met his new housemate on his Cultural Studies course. Yadeen has long dreadlocks and kind eyes - deep brown - that make Jack feel somehow safe. She has just finished making Gungo Pea Soup, and tells him it's one of her favourite things about Jamaica. Her mother is from Kingston, her father Nigerian, so she knows and loves the cooking of both countries.

'I was saving some for the freezer but you look like you need it more,' she says as she spoons the warm-gold mixture into three bowls. Conor finishes bandaging Jack's arm. 'Looks like you've been in the wars,' Yadeen says.

'He had a run in with Billy,' Conor tells her.

'That crazy, crazy boy,' Yadeen says, shaking her head.

'He was always quite odd,' Conor says, 'but after he met you, it got worse. He just shut himself away in his room. Stopped going out. Whenever there was a phone call for him, I'd knock on his door, tell him who it was and, if it wasn't you, he'd yell at me to go away. When he did come out of his room, he was always rushing around, like a speed freak. He hardly spoke to me. If I asked him how things were going between you two, he'd get madly happy. He said he'd be moving out by the end of the year. Said you were going to leave your wife. Said you were going to start looking for a place together. Everything was just a bit too much, too mad. I realised I had to get out.'

'None of what he's told you is true,' says Jack. 'I had a very brief fling with Billy. I ended it with him, and now he won't let it go. He's phoned my house, now he's written

152

to my wife telling her I'm in love with him and I'm going to leave her.'

'Oh dear Lord,' from Yadeen.

'She never saw the letter,' Jack says.

'And he cut you?' Yadeen says. 'The boy's lost his mind.'

Conor has seen it all before. 'Billy is always looking for guys to latch on to. He told me a while back about some guy who had taken him all over the world, a millionaire according to Billy. It was like he was gloating but then it all started to sound a bit too perfect. Billy said the guy was from Toronto and they'd spent a lot of time there. But when I asked if he'd been to the CN Tower, he didn't know what it was.'

'What did he say when you told him you were moving out?' Jack asks.

'He couldn't wait to get rid of me. He said you'd be delighted. He said you wanted to move in as soon as possible and then you'd be looking for something more permanent for the two of you.'

'You're well out of it,' Jack says. Jack doesn't want Conor to end up as collateral damage.

He looks down at his own torn and bloodied shirt. 'I don't suppose you could lend me something to wear?'

'Sure,' Conor says, 'follow me.'

Conor's bedroom is small but tidy. A single bed sits next to the window overlooking the garden - an overgrown rectangle bordered by dilapidated larch lap. A bamboo mat covers most of the floor. The floorboards gently creak underneath. A small pine writing desk is piled high with books on pop art, cubism and communist China. The walls

153

have a velvety bullrush wallpaper peeling off here and there. There's Warhol's soup cans, Keith Haring's *Safe Sex*, and Phil Stern's black-and-white photo of James Dean - lovely eyes peeking over the top of a black crew neck.

A curtained alcove acts as a makeshift wardrobe. At the bottom of the alcove is a plastic storage box containing jeans, socks and underwear.

There is something intimate about being in this room with Conor. He turns his back on Jack, flicking through the clothes in the makeshift wardrobe. The hems of his 501s are turned up rockabilly-style but just a little too far above his Converse All Stars. His heavy-lidded eyes are a very light brown, almost fawn.

'How about this?' He presents Jack with a crushed green lumberjack shirt. 'Should just about fit you.'

'Thanks,' Jack says as he starts undoing the buttons.

It's a little too tight and not Jack's style at all, but no doubt it looks great on Conor. 'How much stuff have you still got to pick up from your old flat?' Jack asks.

'Just a holdall and a pile of college books. God knows where I'm going to put them though.' He looks around the tiny room. Jack laughs.

'I don't think you should go there on your own,' Jack tells him.

'It'll be all right,' he says. 'Billy's a bit weird but he hasn't got it in for me.'

'I'd feel better if I came with you. Just to make sure. Unless there's someone else who can go with you? A boyfriend?'

'I don't have a boyfriend, Jack.'

'Then I should definitely come with you.'

'Billy usually goes to the shops on a Monday, straight after lunch.'

'Monday it is then.'

ii

The zinnias hadn't thrived in the patch I'd chosen for them by the patio. They were starved of light. They made a good metaphor for my relationship with Lizzie. I'd been working hard to hold my marriage together. Now for the first time, the idea of a life without Lizzie seemed a possibility. Perhaps Billy was right. Perhaps I was no good for her. I imagined Thomas grown up, Lizzie and I no longer together, her with another man. I would live alone, of course, keeping my relationships with other men neatly hidden from my ex-wife and son.

My arm was sore so I sat quietly in the garden and downed a large glass of white wine to deaden the pain. I polished off a second glass, savouring its grassy coolness. Not long after that, I heard Lizzie's car return.

'My goodness, what happened to you?'

'A nail in the shed,' I told her.

Another lie, Jack. Hop around the back, Jack. No need to sigh, guy, just tell another lie, Jack. 'It looks worse than it is. I didn't need stitches.'

'Did you go to A&E?'

'I bandaged it myself.'

'How did you manage one-handed?'

'I used my teeth.'

Quick thinking, Jack. A good lie keeps you off the rack, Jack.
'Does it hurt?'

'It's a bit sore.' I held up my empty wineglass. 'But not so bad now.'

'You didn't eat your sandwich.'

'I wasn't hungry - and I was a little preoccupied.'

'You really should eat something. Where's your shirt?'

'I binned it. It was torn and there was a lot of blood.'

'And where did you get this checked thing?' She wrinkled her nose in disgust.

'I picked it up when I got my new suit for work. It was on special offer.' *If you're feeling sly, tell another lie, Jack. You're on top form today.* 'What is this anyway? Twenty questions?' As I threw the comment at her, I knew we were heading for a fight.

'It looks cheap.'

Although she didn't know it, she was criticising Conor, and I despised her for it. 'I could say the same about some of your things.'

She froze for a moment then took a step towards me. 'My *things* are never cheap.'

'And don't I know it?' I shot back. 'We had to remortgage just to keep you in clothes.' I couldn't help myself. I was like a teenage boy whose manhood had been questioned.

'What's got into you?' Both hands were on her hips now. She had that look in her eye reserved for telling off Thomas. 'You've never given a damn about what you wear. It's always jeans and a tee shirt… and the occasional beer-stained jumper.'

'Maybe I'm changing.'

'Well, I look forward to seeing the new you. Or maybe it's not me you're changing for.'

'Meaning?'

156

'I'm still not convinced you haven't got some tart hidden away somewhere, maybe the bottle-blonde infant teacher who started last September. Sandie says you couldn't take your eyes off her.'

'I think you'll find Sandie's talking about Nigel, not me. And it's nice to know you're gossiping behind my back. Thanks for the loyalty.'

'Fuck you, Jack!'

'Very ladylike, Mrs Huntley.' She turned and walked back towards the house. I twisted the wineglass in my hand absent-mindedly. My brain was a little fuddled but my arm had stopped stinging, almost. I considered following Lizzie. I knew I'd have to eventually. Even when I hadn't started an argument, it was always down to me to make the first move.

She looked back at me. 'By the way, you were supposed to drive Thomas over to Lawrence's.' I cursed under my breath. Lawrence was Thomas's best friend and tonight was their sleepover. I made to get up, swayed a little. 'You stay there, Jack,' Lizzie said condescendingly. 'Leave it to the responsible adult. I didn't realise there were two little boys in this family.'

iii

Jack and Conor watch as Billy walks out into the bath-warm sunlight. His shoulders are hunched. He walks in his odd way. Erratic steps. Limbs at slightly awkward angles. His brilliant Icelandic-blond hair makes of him a boy apart. As always.

Billy glances around suspiciously. He weaves his way between parked cars and crosses the street; it's as if he

157

knows he's being watched.

Jack has parked at the top of the street; far enough away not to be seen. He looks at Conor. 'Ready?'

Conor nods uncertainly. Jack thinks maybe Conor is more shaken by all this than he lets on. Billy is many things. Billy is pale as an angel. Billy is a virulence, something you can catch. Billy is violent in a very special way.

Conor turns his key in the front door. The carpet is filthy, edged with grey dust thick as fur. Sweet wrappers glint purple and gold against the carpet's nubby fibres. They go into Conor's room. Jack snatches up Conor's red duffle bag from behind the door. Conor gathers a pile of hardbacks in his arms.

'Wait a minute,' Jack says. For some reason he feels compelled to look in Billy's bedroom.

He pushes the door handle carefully. The click of the mortise sounds like a gun being cocked. Jack isn't prepared for what he sees: blown-up photographs cover the walls; Jack naked; Jack sleeping; Jack erect; pencil sketches of Jack in different sexual positions, and different states of arousal.

The bed is a tangle of sheets and blankets and there, on top, he recognises a pair of his black briefs. The room has that ripe smell of sweat and dirt and boy. Jack's crumpled briefs are stained with white-grey patches; Billy has been masturbating with them.

Jack picks up Billy's 1988 desk diary: ... *and I'm riding Jack like a cowboy at the rodeo and he's smacking my arse with his rough hands until it's raw and stinging. 'I'm done with that fucking bitch,' he shouts out as he ploughs deeper inside me, fucking the cum out of me, then he pulls out, smearing my cum over his own cock and wanking himself off. 'I need you Billy, you're mine, if another man even looks at you, I'll kill him.' He shoots his load over my chest, and rubs it roughly into my skin, marking me with his scent...*

'Christ!'

Conor drops his books at the sound of Jack's voice. As he stoops to pick them up, his hands are trembling.

'Let's just find the negatives and get out of here,' Jack says. They're in a sleek yellow Kodak folder hidden under an assortment of poppers, cock rings, and till receipts. Jack takes the folder then has a change of heart. If Billy finds anything missing, he'll blame Conor, and Jack won't let anything put Conor in harm's way. He puts the folder back where he found it.

'I thought you wanted that.'

'He'll think you took it. He'll come for you.'

The front door slams violently.

Conor jumps. Jack slips past him and peers into the corridor. It's empty. 'Probably just the wind,' he says.

Jack accepts the offer of coffee at Conor's house. 'What are you going to do now, Jack?'

'Go back home. Try to pick up where I left off. Hope Billy got the message this time and leaves me and my family alone.'

'You should have taken the negatives. He can use them against you, blackmail you even.'

159

'I'll just have to get up early every day to catch the postman.' Jack laughs but he's not convincing anyone. 'Does Billy know your address, Conor?'

'I gave it to him so he could send on my mail.'

'Be careful,' Jack says.

Conor scribbles something down on a piece of paper: 'This is my number,' he says, 'just in case you need patching up again.'

*The boy in the BOY London tee shirt
and dark jeans is Billy Soanes, of course.*

chapter twelve

'*BIRMINGHAM ASSAILANTS JAILED*'
Three young men, who were thrown out of a gay night at the Powerhouse Club in Birmingham, launched a vicious attack on an innocent businessman as an 'act of revenge' against homosexuals, a court heard last month.

GAY TIMES, SEPTEMBER 1988

i

Cushions were plumped on sofas and chairs. Crisps and peanuts were poured into bowls. Dips were spooned out of their plastic tubs. Ashtrays were positioned strategically and at regular intervals. Beer cans were put into buckets of ice. Bottles of red wine and soft drinks were neatly arranged on the dining room table. A black rain cloud hovered briefly over the house threatening to wash out the party. An omen, I thought; the sky frowning on the liar, the faker, the man who feigned lust for his wife, the mother of his child. Lizzie's life, her interests, the habits

163

and intrigues of her day were of little more interest to me than elevator music. But that particular cloud had passed with only a little dry thunder. There was no monsoon wedding, only dryness and waiting.

The ungiving sky had turned hazy and the weather was warm enough to lure most of our guests outside.

Lizzie's parents had combined our anniversary party with a weekend stay (on a special deal) at a Mayfair hotel. They had agreed to take Thomas with them after the party so they could spend their Sunday with him in London. And keep him out of our way during the post-party, post-apocalypse cleanup.

I'd just put on a freshly-ironed shirt and a clean pair of chinos when they arrived on the dot as usual. Being ten minutes late for the sake of politeness was lost on my in-laws. Or if they knew the convention, they just ignored it. Sally promptly joined my wife in fussing over the final preparations: dressing green salads, working out timings for the stacks of oven-ready party food, stabbing cocktail sticks into a pointillist sea of green and black olives.

Roy and I took refuge on the patio. I clutched a bottle of beer and did my best to feign interest in First Division football. Then he gave me his layman's view of the Wimbledon final, demolishing a pint of Guinness along the way. In Roy's world, tennis was a game for stuck-up nancy boys. (Although he never said as much to my face.) Underneath it all, we knew we'd never really get along. We were cut from different cloth and we'd both accepted that a long time ago. The result was an uneasy détente; but it was the most either of us could hope for.

It was a relief when Lizzie called me away to welcome

our first real guests.

Bottles were uncorked. Cans tugged open. Chips plucked out of bowls and dunked in their respective dips.

Lizzie's parents rarely saw eye-to-eye with my mother and spoke to her even less. Each side had their own plans for Thomas's future. My mother saw him as a thrusting big shot in the City: a sharp-suited, Porsche-driving, yuppie. Roy and Sally were more interested in moulding a rugged, earthy character, a man's man; and they were no less self-interested than my mother. Roy had already mentioned his ambitions for his grandson in the armed forces. Thomas in the marines! The only common ground they shared was a belief in the unshakeable virtue of traditional, middle-class family values.

Now they sat together self-consciously on a bench next to the water butt, each trying to be more traditional and more middle-class than the other.

Gradually little cliques formed along shared social and/or professional lines: teachers and classroom assistants constituted the largest and most homogenous cohort. They stationed themselves near the French doors, within easy reach of the buffet inside. They were the most boisterous and obtrusive; loud voices carrying across the garden as they trotted in and out of the house with wine glasses topped-up and plates piled high with food.

Thomas and Lawrence, who we'd invited as a happy distraction for Thomas, were racing around the garden, stopping occasionally to gulp Coca-Cola and stuff crisps and chocolate into their mouths. Lizzie and I policed them as best we could.

'No more sweets now, you'll make yourselves sick.' 'Watch where you're going, you'll knock something, or someone, over.'

'Mind that plant pot!'

Lawrence's father, James, worked as a trader at the London Stock Exchange. He'd split recently from Lawrence's mother but he seemed content enough here, oblivious to his son and flirting voraciously with Gemma Alderton, special needs assistant. The eye was drawn - oh yes, it was drawn all right - to her prodigious cleavage by a blouse with frills at the neckline. James inched closer and closer, his bald spot gleaming waxily in the afternoon light. Gemma laughed happily enough at his anecdotes; every bell-like chuckle an opportunity to toss back her head and push out her breasts.

Roy was also watching this little ritual as it played out.

On the periphery of the school group, Nigel looked bored. Sandie, on the other hand, was deep in conversation with Margie, head of Year Three, a stringy middle-aged virago, sipping ginger cordial from a highball glass.

Nigel spotted me and, seeing an opportunity to get away from the raucous teachers, came hurrying over.

'Congratulations, matey,' he beamed. 'Great bash.' He nodded towards Lizzie, ever the consummate hostess, gliding around the garden with a large plate of pizza slices. 'How are you feeling after ten years with the old ball and chain?'

'Very happy,' I told him.

'Got to admire you, mate. You bagged yourself a stunner.'

'Didn't I just? I'm a very lucky man.'

166

'Punching above your weight though. What does a woman like that see in a doughy boy like you? It's a miracle - and a mystery.'

Sandie came over, glancing back across the lawn at the other guests. She stood for a moment weighing up 'special needs' Gemma and her magnificent breasts then winked at me and turned her attention to her husband. Nigel was a lecherous old walrus and I guessed she was thankful he wasn't trying his luck. Yet. She'd soon bring him to heel if she needed to; I'd seen her do it often enough before.

'Pretty good start to the term, wasn't it, Mr Huntley?' she said.

I nodded. 'But I think you've given me a few rotten apples.'

'You're the man to root out the rot,' she said jovially.

In my new class I had to deal with Sean Waller, a freckle-faced thuglet, definitely a gang leader in the making. If the rumours were true, his mother had served time for GBH; and last year she threatened to rip off his form teacher's head and 'shit down her neck'.

Lizzie appeared and her last two slices of pizza were scooped up enthusiastically by Sandie and Nigel.

She looked harassed. 'The wine and beers are running out,' she said as if it were somehow my fault. 'I need you to get more out of the garage.'

'I'll go,' said Nigel. 'You stay here with your good lady wife… and mine.' With a last, quick glance at Gemma Alderton's outstanding bustline, he disappeared around the side of the house.

'You shouldn't be running around like a waitress at your own party,' Sandie said, taking the empty plate from Lizzie

167

and putting it on a garden chair.

'I didn't want the pizzas to get cold,' Lizzie said mechanically.

'I like cold pizza,' I said.

'That's because you're a typical male slob, Mr Huntley,' Sandie laughed.

Lizzie didn't join in.

I could read the signs: she was a perfectionist and the party wasn't perfect and her stress level was climbing too high, too soon.

'Hey!' Nigel beckoned me. 'Your trainee wants you.' I gave him a puzzled look. 'Andy,' he said, 'Andy Church.'

'Oh, I was wondering when he was going to turn up,' Sandie said.

Nigel cast an arm lazily towards the driveway then disappeared into the garage.

ii

The boy in the *BOY London* tee shirt and dark jeans is Billy Soanes, of course.

Most striking of all is his hair, shorn now into a white crew cut which makes him look like an albino gorilla or an undernourished squaddie on the first day of basic training or a novice Carthusian monk facing a life of penitence and silence.

Despite the warm afternoon, I am stone cold.

Billy.

I haul Billy into the house, leading him by the elbow and manoeuvring him into the study.

168

And then he looks at me triumphantly. 'Do you like my new look, Jack?'

And I can't think of anything to say.

'I did it for you.'

And then I hiss: 'What the hell are you doing here? You have no right...'

And 'I have every right,' he says softly. 'It's time now. This is the moment of truth.'

And I say, 'What the fuck are you talking about?' And my heart is hammering in my chest and my balls are riding up into my pelvis, and there's a disturbance at the periphery of my vision like an augur of migraine or madness to come.

And Billy whispers, 'You were in my bedroom,' as he runs his fingers down my chest and he hooks his fingers into my belt buckle and I push him away and he says, 'I know you were there Jack. I could smell you. Then I saw you'd been going through my things and looking at those photos and looking at my underwear. You just can't keep away.' And he begins to giggle in a light sing-song voice; and I wonder if he's taken something because his blue eyes are strangely alight - one slightly more so than the other, as usual - but at the same time they are both oddly opaque, unseeing.

And I spit the words at him, 'Are you fucking crazy?'

And Billy replies coolly, as if all this is the most natural thing in the world, 'Not at all. I've come for you. We can leave together. Right now. On your anniversary. Start again today. It's perfect.'

And I ask, 'How did you even know it was my anniversary?'

'You left the invitations out, right here on the table. I

169

know you did it on purpose. You wanted me to come today, didn't you? You needed me to be your strength, to help you do what you couldn't do on your own.'

And suddenly my anger, like a spark flying above a petrol tank, ignites: 'You fucking little freak!' And I'm struggling to stay in control, to keep from shouting like a madman, alerting the people in the house, in the garden, everyone. I manage to keep the lid on and say, 'Listen to me carefully,' and I have a hammer-heart, and the hammer-hammer-hammer and the runaway feeling are starting to frighten me. I am clinging to a sheer drop and my grip is inadequate; I am falling; and I am saying, 'I am *not* going with you. I am *never* going with you. You are leaving this house and you are never coming back.'

And Billy, well Billy, just stares, you know, because Billy is Billy; and at the same time a-t—t-h-e—s-a-m-e—t-i-m-e something has happened to time itself, something Einsteinian; oceans form; mountains thrust up dead men's hands; fists and fingers of rock; worlds collide and die between one blow of the heart hammering in my chest - hammer-hammer-hammer- and another.

And Billy cocks his head to one side, as if listening to something, and there's that knowing look on his face; halfway between self-assurance and contempt, and his sing-song voice is saying, 'Have it your own way, Jack. You're impossible. But maybe that's why I love you so much.'

I grab his wrists tightly until he cries out. And it feels good to inflict pain on my white ape, my albino squaddie, my little bleached-white novitiate monk; and my face is in his: 'I - DON'T - LOVE - YOU - I - NEVER -

HAVE.' And all he does is laugh, and I can feel that primal fury uncoiling inside. I march him outside past the garage. (Nigel is gone.) I frogmarch him onto The Avenue then into the woods by the golf course, and he is laughing the misplaced, paradoxical laugh of the maniac; and I push him onto the dry dusty earth, and I am overtaken by the primitive desire to despoil: 'If I see your face again,' I snarl, 'I will kill you.'

Billy looks up at me like a bitter and resentful child.

And I pity him.

And I hate him.

iii

I could feel the blood push-pushing in my temples as I walked back to the house. If Billy chose to follow me, there was nothing I could do. I was a convicted man on my way to the gallows, deafened by the susurration of my blood. *You will be taken to a place of execution and hanged by the neck until you are dead.*

The garden was alive with chat and laughing and drinking and eating. A lovely Saturday afternoon. And it could all be over in a few brief seconds. Oh, the elasticity of time. I stopped and turned slowly to look behind me. But Billy wasn't there. I walked back a few steps to get a better view of The Avenue and the woods. No sign of the white hair, of my white mantis of a *Boy London*. He'd dissolved into shadow. And I really did pray it was for good.

But I couldn't shake the feeling he was playing with me like a John Wayne Gacy - why wouldn't he? - taking me to the brink of despair until I would beg for him to finish me once and for all. I took a deep breath and crouched down on my haunches until the waves of nausea subsided then I went into the kitchen and poured a glass of wine and drank it straight down.

'Daddy! Daddy!' Thomas came racing in, Lawrence close behind him. 'Can I show Lawrence my fort and toy soldiers?' I nodded, and the boys raced up the stairs.

I found Sandie and Nigel back outside. 'Thanks for fetching the booze,' I said.

'No problem, pal.' Nigel slapped me on the back. He looked jauntily at Sandie. 'It's the bloody teachers who're drinking you out of house and home.' Sandie rolled her eyes at him then she changed the subject.

'We may need to dip into the reserve budget before Christmas, Jack,' she said.

'You're probably right.' I usually agreed with Sandie. 'The playground has to be resurfaced - it won't last another winter.'

'Honestly you two,' Nigel scolded us. 'It's a lovely Saturday afternoon and you're talking shop.'

'Sorry darling,' Sandie said. 'It's just I so rarely get to speak to this man at work. He always seems to be running around busy with something. Or maybe he's just hiding away from me.'

'More like sorting some problem in Year Six,' I said. 'X has thumped Y or stabbed them with a compass or stolen their Top Trumps.'

'Rather you than me, matey,' Nigel said. 'Anyway, why don't we all just agree to talk about…'

His voice trailed off. I saw his lips moving but no more sound came out.

172

Sandie put her hand to her mouth.

Everything fell silent as if the volume had been turned down.

iv

It is Billy, walking across the lawn towards me. And his arms are outstretched in silent supplication. And he is crying silently. And he is Saint Sebastian with blood falling from the puncture wounds at his wrists. And he is partially naked. And he is a wounded creature, something run through, arrow-struck. And the blood is falling relentlessly and he is advancing just as relentlessly towards me. And his face is the hollowed-out face of a martyr, rudderless on the Mediterranean Sea. And he drops to his knees in front of me. And here is a new obscenity – his face is level with my crotch. And there is blood everywhere. And he is the shaven-headed pilgrim flayed by the long march along the Way of Saint James, one of the three great pilgrimages of Christendom, to that Galician glory, Santiago de Compostela. He is a bloodied martyr come to see the relic bones of the Apostle James. And now he is on his knees before the bone. He is a postulant before the image of Christ. And I have the bone. And I am the Christ. Chino-Christ. Cock-Christ, his defiler. And he is speaking very quietly. And he is calling on me to do something. And he is fallen on his knees and he is calling softly: 'Help me, Jack. Please, help me.' And time is collapsing again – the drop of water is f-a-l-l-i-n-g – and every part of me shrinks back from this palest of all wraiths. Every part of me draws away from this bloodied wraith with the mismatched blue eyes

173

beseeching my chino-covered cock to do something. And every part of me shrinks away from Billy, except one, and I would fuck him before God and the assembled company, a great retribution of a fuck for ruining my life.

Margie Attwell approaches Billy in the tenderest way imaginable, holding two white hand towels like shrouds or priestly vestments.

Now she is wrapping fragments of the Turin Shroud around Billy's wrists to staunch the flow of wine-dark blood.

The dearly beloved are crowding around to see more clearly and Sandie is telling them to stand back, to give the martyr some air.

Billy, martyred in blood and semen.

'Who is he?' Lizzie asks with her hand to her forehead as if about to cross herself.
'Andy Church,' Nigel says.
'That's not Andy Church,' Sandie says.
Nigel looks at me. 'Who is it then, Jack?'
'Do you know this boy?' Lizzie's voice folds over on itself and I lose it in the *push-blood, push-blood* sound in my ears. I wonder, dimly, if this is what the beginning of a heart attack feels like.
'Of course he does,' Nigel says. 'He came over when you were away.' *Push-blood. Push-blood. Push-blood.* I hear Margie a very long way off, telling someone to ring for an ambulance.

'Who the hell is he?' Lizzie's voice rises. 'Tell me!'

I cannot look at her. I am the great Chino-Christ. Cock-Christ, the boy's defiler.

'Is he going to be all right?' I mutter to Margie.

'If we can get him to a hospital,' she says. 'The bleeding is slowing down.'

'Who is he Jack?' Lizzie whispers. Her mother has an arm around her. Sandie is at her side. Everyone looks at me and I have to decide, will I deny him? Will it be three times before the cock crows? Co-co-rico, co-co-rico, co-co-rico.

'I do know him,' I say and I am no Saint Peter, no Rock. I am naked, revealed, a holy, or unholy revenant detached from the man once called Jack Huntley. 'I need to go with him to the hospital now and I'll tell you everything later.'

v

Billy is lying silently in the white brilliance of the examination room. He is smaller and paler than he's ever looked before; more of an emphatic whiteness than a person.

Posters announce the terrible risks of rabies - 'la rage' - and AIDS.

Billy has crossed over to sedation's other world. He stares at me groggily, trying to focus on my face, then drifts away again to the unimaginable other-place of his origins. And there is a stark elegance about him now, the profound and tormented beauty of psychological unravelling. In this moment, he is silently, luminously mad.

And even though we are together in this small room, I feel intolerably alone.

175

There are no words to describe how much I regret those first few stolen days with Billy.

I see again the stunned faces at the party; there again, the terrible silence, the volume turned right down. Who knew so much could be said by saying nothing? Lizzie started to cry, and I tried to touch her, to console her, and she slapped my hand aside, and then her mother and Sandie hurried her away into the house and I saw Roy Burgess stamp his foot like an angry bull, muscles popping in his jaw.

I sat on the porch with Margie and Billy and we waited for the ambulance. Billy rested his head against my shoulder and Margie looked uneasily into the distance.

I tried to be still. I wondered how still is it possible for one man to be? I tried to be still, to be a non-thing. Little by little, it felt as if I would cast no shadow. I was nothing staring at nothing and nothing was staring back, and then the sound of the siren wrenched me into the moment. I insisted Margie go back to the party; she walked away without a word, without looking at me. An eerie quiet had descended over the house, like the cloying stillness in the air before a monster storm.

I rode in the ambulance with Billy. As I looked back towards the house, Roy was standing blackly in the driveway.

Now Billy started calling my name. The ambulance man told him he was going to be okay; told him to lie still, told him he just had to try and stay calm.

'Mr Huntley?' The junior doctor looked like he'd been on duty for a hundred hours. Maybe he had. 'Are you any relation to Mr Soanes?'

'No,' I said. 'I'm just a friend.'

'Do you know how we can contact his next of kin?'

'No, I don't. Is he going to be all right?'

'Yes,' the doctor brightened. The news was good, not bad. 'It looks much worse than it is. We've stitched him up and given him some painkillers. He'll be fine. Physically.'

'His old flatmate is on his way,' I said, shifting my feet. 'He might be able to tell you about his next of kin.'

I'd phoned Conor as soon as we got to the hospital. I'd never been so glad to hear anyone's voice. I felt overwhelming relief that he was coming. The thought of Conor made me feel less alone.

'Thank you, Mr Huntley,' the doctor said.

'Are you keeping Billy in?'

'There's no bed, I'm afraid. But I'll give you a prescription for more painkillers and you can always call us if you're worried. Make sure you're careful with the painkillers, though. Only give Billy two at a time, for obvious reasons. You can take him home once he wakes up properly. Just inform the nurse on duty and she'll discharge him.'

It seems a very long wait before Conor arrives. He hugs Jack tightly as if they are the lone survivors of some unspeakable tragedy, which, in a way, they are.

'I'm so sorry this has happened, Jack,' he says. 'I never thought he'd do something like this.'

'I'm really glad you're here.'

Conor smiles.

'I don't know what to do,' Jack says, 'they're going to discharge him.'

'It's okay,' says Conor gently, 'we can take him back to mine. There's a spare room and Yadeen's a first aider.'

'Thank you,' Jack whispers. He realises they are still holding on to each other. Instinctively he turns to look at Billy. Billy is watching them both with his blank mismatched eyes.

*'And you've been screwing that boy, haven't you?
That revolting little nancy boy.'*

chapter thirteen

i

Five minutes to midnight: an unearthly time - a fallow field of time between the end of one day and the beginning of the next. Everything is slowing down - the Einsteinian thing again - sixty lifetimes an hour - and Jack is on the outside of the floating world, an alien observer looking through a microscope at all of the life in a drop of water. He sits in Conor's kitchen, drinking coffee and anticipates his return to Claia Bourne: Lizzie pacing up and down, Thomas staring sleepily, 'Daddy, where did you go?' At least Thomas was playing upstairs when the martyr fell on the last steps of his corrosive pilgrimage.

Jack knows Thomas will be looked after. He doesn't want to see him pulling the covers over his head, frightened by the sound of shouting downstairs. Roy and Sally should have taken Thomas with them by now as they had planned. Lizzie could rant and rave all she liked and probably was ranting and raving with Sandie, audience of one. Going back now would probably do more harm than good. Best to stay away. However bad things are, he told himself, they always look better in daylight.

He wonders what Nigel is thinking, then decides he doesn't want to know; he can't face his friend's revulsion or disgust.

He has to deal with Billy somehow. He has to find a way to keep Billy out of all their lives. But he has no idea how.

So he sits in the kitchen at Conor's house, drinking black coffee, and recounting the afternoon's events. His voice is hoarse as he relives those awful moments: the puncture wounds at Billy's wrists; Billy's stigmata, those bloody signs of his crucifixion at Jack's hands; Lizzie breaking down; the stunned silence from the people he'd known for years; the distaste written on his friends' faces.

Conor lets him talk.

Footsteps on the stairs and then Yadeen's voice. 'Billy's sleeping,' she says. 'He won't wake up till morning.'

'Thanks for everything you've done,' Jack says. 'I'm sorry to have brought this to your door.'

'It's just life doing its mischief,' she says. She declines Conor's offer of a coffee. 'I'm off to bed. I'm on the last pages of *Beloved* and I want to finish it tonight.' Conor takes Jack's cup gently from him and puts it on the draining board.

'You look shattered,' he says. 'I'd better show you our guest facilities.' In the living room he unfolds the sofa bed. 'This is as good as it gets.'

'It'll be fine. Thank you for helping. I really appreciate it. You're a life saver. You and Yadeen.'

'She's a good girl,' Conor says. Jack holds his gaze. At a different time, he would have thought about kissing him. But here he is in darkness at the edges of the luminous world and there is already too much madness here.

Conor shifts a little bashfully. 'Better let you get some sleep,' he says.

'I'm not looking forward to tomorrow.'

'You'll get through it.'

The bed is uncomfortable. The mattress is thin and lumpy and worn out by too many students, too many parties. He doesn't draw the curtains. He doesn't want to be confronted by the pitch dark in an unfamiliar room. From time to time, a car headlight rakes over the grubby net curtains and reminds him of where he is and how he came to be there. *The bedroom is dark. The boy follows the man into the bedroom and the man and the boy begin to undress. Slowly they reveal themselves to each other. The man stands naked, priapic now before the boy. The boy's slender body is pale like Carrara marble. His pubic hair is soft and blond. He is very blond. He is the blondest boy the man has ever seen. He looks at the man with peculiar eyes. It is as if he is looking into the world from somewhere unimaginable.* Jack is weeping softly in the dark. For what might have been. For what is lost. For the roads not taken. For the mystery of love. *Billy.* Dread battles his exhaustion, and he is awake hour after dismal hour. He realises he is the one who has fallen. How long can one man suffer the hour? How long is an hour? Who can say with any certainty? How much suffering can the hour contain? *Billy.* Now the hour is by

183

Jack's side like a dog that will not be shaken off. Jack is haunted by time.

Saint Sebastian is a wounded creature, run through, arrow-struck.
The flow of wine-dark blood lessens.
'Who is he?' Lizzie asks with her hand to her forehead.
My shaven-headed pilgrim flayed by the long march along the Way of Saint James.
'Who is he Jack?' Lizzie whispers.
My bloodied martyr come to see the relic bones of the Apostle James.
Co-co-rico, co-co-rico, co-co-rico.

And finally. Merciful oblivion.

ii

Conor is sitting in the armchair opposite Jack. Jack sits up, squinting in the light.

'You still look totally knackered,' Conor says.

'I lay awake for a long time.'

Conor makes tea. Jack keeps an eye on the bacon under the grill. The rashers crackle and sizzle and pop lightly and this is the most normal thing in the world. This kitchen. Breakfast. Jack takes the scorching bacon from under the grill. Conor nudges the rashers with a fork onto the slices of bread and the thick butter melts and runs on contact. Conor cuts the sandwich in two and gives half to Jack.

Then.

'You devious fucker!' Billy is standing in the doorway, staring at Conor. 'You dirty little cheat!'

'Hey!' Jack says.

Billy.

Jack positions himself between Billy and Conor. Jack says, 'There's nothing going on here.'

'Liars! Both of you.'

Billy is shouting obscenities. Nothing quite makes sense. Billy runs at Conor but Jack manages to grab him around the waist and holds him off as best he can, and Billy is kicking and screaming insults, and hurling his fists at Conor, and he is preternaturally, devilishly strong.

But then something else of an entirely different nature enters the room. Yadeen is at Billy's side.

Yadeen is speaking very softly. She is reassuring him; her words are Jamaican Creole.

Softest Patwah.

Jack feels Billy's body relax. Yadeen's words are like music: *Deh yah, mi deh yah, wi deh yah.* (And the old spirits are at work.)

Yadeen continues in English: 'You've been through a terrible shock. All this excitement is doing you no good. You need to rest. You understand me?' After a few moments Billy nods simply.

Jack feels the fight go out of him.

'That's right, darling,' Yadeen says. 'You're going to need something for the pain. Your cuts must be hurting like the Devil, getting you all anxious and upset.'

She tells Conor to get the sedatives from her room. A few minutes later, Billy is back in bed, staring at all three

185

of them with heavy-lidded eyes.

'He'll be all right now,' Yadeen says.

iii

Claia Bourne seemed a different place. Bad memories and shadows of other lives, and shapes in the dark. I opened the door to silence; the panelled hallway was dark and remarkably cold. The house itself was watching, absolutely without pity. Every room was a pristine accusation: ashtrays emptied and scrubbed; tabletops polished; the draining board gleaming; every piece of glassware and crockery back in its proper place. The party and its echoes wiped clean away. Lizzie must have been up all night, washing and tidying away all trace of yesterday, washing and tidying away all trace of me. She always cleaned when she was angry or upset. A symbolic ritual; *I will wash away this stain, this hurt*; like Hindus bathing in the Ganges during the holy days of the Kumbh Mela. Here all sins are cleansed. Here all mistakes are atoned for.

My beautiful boys from *Mister* were there on the table, torn limb from limb - a stark tangle of cocks and come-to-bed eyes, piled high; my wicked books ready for burning. I could have wept for my ruined boys and for my ruined self. I had been discovered and I was lost - all in one go.

(The moment began to stretch out like a bead of water falling in slow motion.)

'I found this filth in the shed,' Lizzie said. She had not put on her makeup and her face was pale and drawn.

186

Here was the final martyrdom.

'I started to think about how strange you've been lately,' she said. 'How evasive. Then I remembered what the doctor said… about that drug, about homosexuals using it. Your nasty little sex drug put our child in the hospital. He was in hospital because of you, Jack!'

I realised she hated me.

She folded her arms before going on. 'So I went rooting about and I found all your disgusting magazines. You're a pervert! A bugger! A dirty queer!'

She was sobbing and I took her in my arms as kindly as I could.

'I want to hear you say it!' she shouted, catching her breath. 'Tell me to my face you're a queer.'

I couldn't speak. All that life. All the beauty. All that hope. All that hiding. All that desire.

She drew away from me as if I were infectious. 'Tell me!' she said. She was shaking with rage. 'Say it!'

I just looked at her.

'You're a coward,' she said bitterly and she was not wrong. 'You're not a man. You're pathetic. You make me sick to my stomach. And you've been screwing that boy, haven't you? That revolting little nancy boy. Where did you do it, Jack? In our bed? I want you gone. Get out of this house and don't come back. I never want to see you again.'

'I'm so sorry, Lizzie,' I managed to whisper. 'I'm so very sorry.'

'Get out!' she spat the words, pointing to the door.

'Where's Thomas?' I asked.

She folded her arms again, almost triumphantly now, her eyes narrowing. 'Where you can't get your filthy hands on him.'

187

'Is he okay? I want to see him.'

'But I don't want you to see him. Now get out.'

'Lizzie…'

'Get out Jack!'

iv

I drove around familiar streets now oddly foreign. Suburbia had become another country. I was the alien thing, the stranger in a strange land. Like all men worthy of the name, I was addicted to sex. And I hated myself for it, hated myself for being this slave to the all-consuming need to fuck and dominate. Slave to that particular rhythm. All men, a pack of dogs, wolf men with no conscience, no compass at all. I drove as far as Epping Forest where whispering woodlands fringe London's miles of concrete, where suburbia can't quite encroach on the kingdom of the Green Man. I remembered my mother bringing me here, long summers ago: woodland walks in dappled light. A remote place where nothing could touch me. Kingdom of childhood. No mortgage. No responsibility. No wife. No sex. The only expectation: to look and be wonder-filled, and to play.

I pulled up and killed the engine. It was blissfully silent inside the car. I realised part of me was relieved to have been discovered, at last. My fabulous secret was out. I was free. What I had dreaded for so long had happened. My life - my old life - was in ruins. My relationship with Billy had brought me low. One sugar-sweet moment, and now the inescapable fall into the pit where the boy *is sitting on a scarlet beast that was full of blasphemous names, and it had seven heads and ten horns. The boy was clothed in purple and scarlet and adorned with gold and jewels and pearls, holding in his hand a golden cup full of abominations and the impurities of his prostitution.* And I am burned up, consumed, but also made clean in the pit's unholy fires.

The gentle approach of autumn scented the air. Other people were walking the same path, people with dogs, couples laughing, parents hand-in-hand with their children. I looked at humanity and humanity looked back at me: a man with an odd air, on his own in the woods. No pet to walk, no wife, no girlfriend, no kids. Humanity watched as I passed by, condemning me silently - or that's how it felt - as an incipient rapist, imminent paedophile, pervert in their presence. My marriage was a dying thing. I hadn't been able to say the words, to be clear, to be out, to admit to Lizzie, 'I am gay'. And I had told so many lies along the way. An Olympiad of lies. It had taken a great container-tanker of lies to bring me to this point.

It wouldn't take much for Lizzie to make sure I never saw Thomas again.

No court would place a child with a father like me.

She'd have the backing of every lawyer, priest and moralist in the county.

What I felt was grief. Plain, hollowing grief. I could end it all now. Wouldn't that be a great big 'fuck you' to life, the universe and everything?

But a man is more than himself. I am at least adult

enough to acknowledge that. Our lives are not our own. I couldn't do that to Lizzie; I couldn't do it to Thomas.

I couldn't face my friends; they had seen Billy stricken; they had heard Billy call me by my name, like a lover. I had nowhere to go. I was alone. Once you're on the floor, at least, there is nowhere further to fall.

When I got back to the car, I sat for a long time. Then I turned the key in the ignition and the engine rippled into life.

v

'Billy's gone,' Conor tells Jack simply.

All the world's unravelling. 'What happened?'

Yadeen picks up the story: 'I was out in the back yard, and I heard a terrible racket so I ran inside, and Billy was shouting and wailing and trashing Conor's room. When he saw me, he had the Devil's own eyes and he punched me and kicked me and I swear *mi fraid the duppy ah come.* The Devil's in him now and then, just as suddenly, he was gone. I don't ever want to see that boy again. True.'

'I was at the shops when it all broke loose,' Conor says.

'Where would Billy go?' Jack asks. 'Home?'

Conor still has a key to Billy's flat. He and Jack find the place much the same as before, only worse. The stench of rotting food is overwhelming, exactly as if something has been martyred and died. Conor opens the windows and carefully empties the stinking contents of the rubbish bin. There's something akin to love in the care he takes, washing the bin with soapy water and putting it neatly back in the corner of the kitchen. A little order re-enters the chaos; Conor is a thoughtful boy.

There is no Billy to be seen, no fury from another world, only this thoughtful, careful boy and the air agitating the curtains in Billy's absence; and everything is space and air and peace and care where Billy is not.

Jack and Conor drive slowly along the surrounding streets, cruising the curbs like American cops in a 1970s made-for-TV movie. But this isn't America and it isn't a movie and there's no sudden sign of Billy, no screaming tyres, no rubber burned into the road, no car chase. Conor and Jack are simply defeated. They find nothing. They are not sure what to do next. They are deflated and solemn and hungry.

Harry's Place is a straightforward workmen's cafe with no-nonsense furniture and steamed-up windows, come winter, come summer. They order egg and chips twice and sit with two large mugs of builders' tea. Jack tells Conor he is out on his own now, has nowhere to go. 'At least, there's no further to fall,' he shrugs.

They drink their tea, the colour of tar.

'You can stay at ours for now,' Conor says. 'Do you think things'll ever go back to normal? Do you think she'll take you back?'

'Who wants to be married to a gay guy?'

'Another gay guy.' Conor laughs, trying to lighten Jack's mood.

'I might never see my son again.'

'She'll come round in the end,' Conor says. 'You are his

father, after all.'

'That won't count for much in court.'

'It might not come to that. I can't pretend to know what you're going through, but it can't help imagining the worst.'

Sitting with Conor in this neat East End diner, lifts Jack's spirits a little. The air is clearer. The rotting smell has been washed away.

But tomorrow is Monday and he can't face going into school and the thought of ringing Sandie brings him low again, the awful things she's likely to say; the whole great mess of it.

Back at Conor's, he steels himself and dials her number.

'Jack? How are you?' She's less guarded than he expected. 'How's Lizzie?'

'Things are really not good.'

'I'm sorry to hear that.' She's carefully noncommittal.

Jack hates asking for time off; he always feels like a shirker. 'Everything's a terrible mess and I'm not feeling too great…'

'Jack,' she cuts in, 'unless I hear from you I won't expect you in all week.'

He is relieved, and grateful for this simple act of kindness.

'That seemed fairly straightforward,' Conor says as Jack replaces the receiver.

'Yeah, let's go and tidy up your room.'

The duvet has been slashed; there are feathers

everywhere like fallen snow, the kind of snow that falls on all the living and all the dead in a Dublin graveyard.

Jack thinks of the phrase 'spitting feathers' and pillow fights and a goose at Christmas but that is all a very long time ago.

Conor's clothes have been cut or torn and thrown across the room. His books have been spoiled, pages ripped, spines with broken backs like so many broken bodies; first they come for the books, then they come for you. Conor and Yadeen smile out of a photograph with the sea behind them and the sun in their eyes; and the point of a slim, flexible filleting blade punctures the paper between Conor's eyes. Oh the Furies are let loose now: 'endless anger', 'jealous rage', and 'vengeful destruction' are free and a-hunting in the mundane world; that's how Virgil would have it. Jack knows it. Jack sees the phantom Billy; beautiful boy-wraith lost to the duppy, to the shadow spirits of Jamaica, to madness.

Mischief and madness.

Jack puts his arms around Conor. 'You're not staying here tonight.'

The suitcase slipped out of my hand and down the stairs, emptying its contents onto the floor.

chapter fourteen

i

The Alfred Hitchcock Hotel honours that most famous of east London's sons. The interior with its wood-panelling reminds Jack just a little too much of Claia Bourne but there's a good log fire to make the place welcoming and the bar is cosy enough. Photograph's from the great man's films decorate the walls: Janet Leigh screaming her head off in the shower; Tippi Hedren having her hair torn out by *The Birds*. There's Hitch's birth certificate: 'thirteenth August 1899, Alfred Joseph, boy'; there's his certificate of marriage to Alma Lucy Reville dated 1926.

Jack's room is on the first floor, reached by a narrow corridor. The lock clicks dully as he turns the key. There is a strange tenor to this moment. In what way is this moment significant? *When one door closes, another opens*. Or other platitudes people repeat to make themselves feel better. Tender shoots of a new beginning. Perhaps. The

195

door opens onto a small, simply furnished room. A large window looks out over Leyton Flats, that 'scenic and tranquil' nature reserve of ancient woodland, 'ideal for picnicking and boating in summer'. A rose-pink pair of lungs for the people of east London.

Jack knows the Hitchcock from before. He and Sandie held the staff Christmas dinner there last year. It was good value; the people were friendly enough; the cooking was 'traditional pub' and the helpings were large.

Jack had suggested it might be better if Yadeen stayed away from home as well, at least for a little while. He'd offered to pay, but she said she preferred to stay put: it was her home and she wasn't going to be displaced by *yuh duppy man*. Nevertheless, she asks her brother to stay with her for a few nights.

It feels very important to get Conor away; Billy knows where Conor lives; Billy knows how to hurt people. Conor is more rattled than he's prepared to admit and Jack feels - and Jack is - responsible. He throws the keys onto the bedside table and doesn't know if he's miserable or relieved or both and, apart from any of that, he has a headache coming.

'Are you okay?' asks Jack's careful, thoughtful boy.

'I don't know. Yes, I'm okay. I'm getting a headache.'

'Take your shirt off and lie on the bed.'

Conor kneads Jack's trapezius muscles with smooth, careful movements. Next he pushes his palms slowly and firmly along either side of Jack's spine working up into his neck and cranium. Conor seems to know what he's doing. Jack lets him continue for a few more minutes and the pain in his head starts to dissipate. Jack pulls him close and kisses him gently.

They both lie very still. There is only the sound of their breathing.

Jack lifts Conor's tee shirt carefully over his head and Conor looks up, as if he is about to ask a question, and Jack peels off Conor's 501s with infinite tenderness and places his hand over the front of Conor's white briefs, feeling him swell gently, and he teases the waistband down carefully and the boy's youthful masculinity rises, and now Jack is running his fingers slowly over the soft velvet of Conor's skin. Now he is on top of Conor, naked except for the gold chain at his neck, which hangs loosely down, swaying in careless rhythm as his hardness answers the boy's and Conor closes his eyes and rests his hands lightly on Jack's shoulders; and Jack moves in and out of him, slowly and, yes, lovingly, and they are skin to skin and Conor is working himself, and there, there is the sudden warm torrent and Conor's belly is streaked with lustrous white and Jack is overwhelmed by his own release so that his body jolts and shudders and surrenders and they fall together, entangled, as the daylight fades.

And they are both still hard, a beautiful aching hardness on the borders of bliss and pain.

Jack watches the boy's stalk bob and dance as he dresses. He watches Conor check his hair intently in the mirror, coaxing it into place with small careful strokes in that lovely way boys do. Jack wants to know him as he knows himself. He wants to know what Conor dreams of, what

197

he hopes for from life, and what he fears. He may even allow himself to love him.

And somewhere far off Billy is lost. Will they ever see Billy again?

At the same time, something new is afoot, as if the entire world were turning on gears and this change, this new alignment, has the weight of the earth herself behind it. The Furies are met by something else. 'Endless anger', 'jealous rage', and 'vengeful destruction' are met by the strange complicity of the cosmos when there is love, when love, that ineffable, ungraspable, unfathomable thing, is unexpectedly present.

ii

'You're not a homosexual. You're a confirmed bachelor.' My mother's face was a study of bullish denial with a dash of desperation thrown in. She sucked her lips into a thin line, blinking rapidly as if woken from some terrible dream. She seemed to take my coming out as a direct challenge, something I'd chosen to do *to her* out of spite.

This was much harder than my run-in with Lizzie. Lizzie had put two and two together and taken the lead in confronting me. With my mother I'd had to begin the conversation, choose my moment, find the right way to confess who I really was. As if there was ever a 'right' way.

Above all I had to say the words: *I'm gay.* Those words, when they came, didn't sound like me. I wondered if I'd ever get used to the label and all its connotations.

'It's that girl.' My mother seized any opportunity to

criticise Lizzie. 'She's made you like this with all her hoity-toity ways. She's got you all messed up.'

She fiddled with her brooch as she always did when a plan was forming in her mind. 'This thing you think you're like.' (She couldn't say the word 'gay'.) 'You're just confused. You aren't one of those people. It's not true.'

'It is true,' I said quietly, looking down at my muddy brogues.

'No it isn't.' Her answer was swift and percussive like a teacher reacting to a wayward pupil. 'You are not a homosexual.' The armour was back on. The barricades were manned. I waited to hear what she was going to say next. She always had a strategy - a strategy to get me into a decent college, a strategy to get me the 'right' girl, a strategy for my son and his future, regardless of his wishes. Or mine.

'We'll fight her,' she said. 'I'll support you every step of the way. We'll get Thomas away from her. We'll find a good lawyer. We can go and speak to someone this week. She's not getting hold of my grandson.'

'We don't need to get into a fight about anything,' I said slowly, picking my words carefully. 'I don't want Thomas caught in the middle.' She looked at me like I'd just stepped out of a flying saucer.

Take me to your leader.

'Are you telling me you're not going to fight for your son?'

'Lizzie is his mother. If it comes to it, the courts are going to give her custody. I just want to be able to see him.' I emphasised the words: '*If it comes to it.*'

'Do you think for one minute she'll let you? We need to make the first move. You're in the professions, you're a deputy head. That's got to count for something.'

She began pacing up and down. She was relishing the idea of putting Lizzie in her place. She'd been wanting to do it for such a long time. 'You'll have to move in with me, that'll look better. Take the focus away from your little indiscretion.'

'Stop it!' I said so forcefully she flinched. 'I don't want any of this.' Her sudden surprise evaporated just as quickly. She wasn't going to take me seriously; I was not a man in her eyes; I was a child and I needed to be organised; sorted out; straightened out.

'We'll see,' she said. 'I'll clear out the spare room. You can bring your stuff over this afternoon.'

'I'm not going to move in with you.'

'Where are you staying anyway?' It was the first time she'd thought to ask; she'd been so focused on the fantasy of her son, the well-regarded family man, and her grandson the high-powered yuppie-in-the-making.

'I'm staying at a hotel.'

'Check out. It's much better that you're with me. You don't want to look like some useless drifter.'

'I'm with someone.' (And there it was - very quietly and very tenderly, the sound of the earth, the great mother earth turning. And there - the sanction of the cosmos because love was present, and for a moment it sounded like children in the streets singing.)

'Have you gone mad?' She gave me 'her look'. It had the power to shrink me down to nothing when I was five and it had the same power over me now. I was cut down, nothing. I thought she was going to grab me, and shake me. 'You can't see any girls until everything is finalised and we've got custody of Thomas.'

'It's not a girl,' I said. Then, after a few seconds: 'His name is Conor.'

'No!' She spat the words out into the air. 'I do not want to hear this. You are not like that. You're not one of those people. I won't have it!'

I bought a bottle of Glenfiddich on my way back to the Hitchcock. Conor wasn't there, and I was afraid for a moment and then I remembered he'd gone to the poly for a meeting with his tutor. The room seemed piteously small, and drab all of a sudden; a stark reminder of what my life had become. I wondered if I had it in me to start again. I didn't know if I had the imagination or the courage to make a new life, by which I meant the strength of character. I began drinking. Then when the alcohol started to take effect, I thought about how things might have been different. The booze made me maudlin and I was soon wallowing in self-pity. I started punishing myself. What an idiot I had been. What a non-thing, a nonsense I was. I kept at it until I no longer recognised the accusing voice inside my own head. Oh, but in the streets the children were singing.

iii

When Conor gets back, Jack is in a terrible state: he is frankly, fulsomely drunk, and weeping, and it is a measure of his trust in Conor - or his drunkeness - that he doesn't try to hide his tears. He has given up pretending.

Conor gently takes the bottle from him. Conor says nothing. He just holds Jack, and Jack feels the reassuring heat of his body, and he weeps again. They lie together on

the bed in silent understanding as Jack drifts off into the
black.

iv

I thought I'd find Lizzie at home but the house was
empty. I had the unshakeable feeling that the walls had
something to say. Lizzie probably couldn't bear to be under
the same roof but we'd have to see each other sometime.
Things had to be faced and decided; no longer as man and
wife planning a future, but as refugees from a failed
marriage. I went into Thomas's room. I missed him and it
was like a physical pain. His toys were jumbled carelessly
together: his Etch A Sketch, his View-Master, his Rock
'em Sock 'em Robots. Next to his night light was the photo
of us: father and son. He has a Mr Whippy 99 and his
face is smeared with melted ice cream and chocolate
flakes. We'd chased down what seemed like every street in
Truro. It was a baking day and we couldn't find the ice
cream van, though we could hear the squawky, high-
pitched chimes. The simple sweetness of the memory
hollowed me out. I don't know how long I sat on the floor,
looking at that picture. I was wishing I could transport us
all back to that day by force of will. Would I do things
differently if I could go back and start again? That's one
of life's great questions, isn't it? Would I still live a lie?
Would I still sleep with Billy Soanes? I didn't know. All I
knew was that I wanted to see my little boy. I wondered if
I'd ever see him again while he was still a child. Maybe I'd
be forced to wait till the day the child was a man with a
wife and children of his own, and I would go looking for
him; perhaps I'd have the courage to tell him who I was,

and explain why I'd failed him. Or maybe my resolve would falter and I'd watch from a distance for a while then disappear again, unable to face him.

It took a huge effort to leave his little room and go to my own bedroom, our bedroom. Everything was as it always was. It was just a normal day at Claia Bourne but there was also something treacherous about the normality. It was a lie obscuring something else. I packed a suitcase, hurriedly folding shirts, trousers, socks and underwear; and threw my toilet bag on top. Then I heard the front door open. *Damn it!* I didn't have the stomach for another fight with my wife. I shut the case and hurried out of the room and Roy Burgess was standing at the foot of the stairs.

'You better have packed everything you need in that case,' he said, 'because you're never coming back here again.'

'This is my house too,' I said. He barred my way and I hesitated, uncertain what he wanted from me. Then he grabbed me by the throat. His move was very sudden, like a mamba taking a bird. He slammed me against the wall. I banged my head very hard. He squeezed his thick fingers around my windpipe, steadily crushing it.

'I don't think you understand me, sunbeam.' He bared his teeth just like a dog. 'I said, you are *never* coming back.' He was retribution in the shape of a man. He was compressing my throat so violently, I pictured the skin tearing and his hands red with my viscera. 'You are going to get in your car, and go. And later on, you are going to sign all the necessary papers to make sure my daughter and my grandson have what they need. But you are never coming near them again. Either of them.'

I started to lose consciousness; the suitcase slipped out of my hand and down the stairs, emptying its contents onto the floor. 'Do you understand me?' he snarled. The walls were bowing inwards. I clawed feebly at his arm, but his arm was made of iron. He spoke again and this time his voice sounded deeper, slower: 'I said, do you understand me?' I managed to nod and he let me go. Waves of vertigo mounted up against me, like the tide mounting up against a sea wall, and somehow I managed to get everything back into the case without fainting. Roy stood over me and I knew I must not lose consciousness or fall; I knew that falling would provoke him.

'There was something off about you the day I met you,' he said. 'I was right all along. From now on you keep away from my daughter and my grandson. You're a lousy little ponce. A shirt-lifter. A dirty little arse bandit.'

Conor leans forward and rests his beer on the table.
'I saw Billy today,' he says bluntly.

chapter fifteen

'*GALOP REPORT HIGHLIGHTS POLICE HOSTILITY*'
*Police in London have been accused of 'indifference',
'hostility', 'unprofessionalism' and 'sheer incompetence' in their
dealings with gay men in the capital. The accusations are
levelled in the annual report from GALOP, the Gay London
Policing Group.*
GAY TIMES, JANUARY 1989

i

Billy.
A face glimpsed on a crowded London street. The
wraith has come.

An oddly beautiful boy in a gay club, dancing jaggedly
- that's the word - under the strobe lights.

In the distance, a flash of oh-so-pale blond hair.

I am haunted by illusions and allusions, by tricks of the
light and the mind. Is this the beginning of psychosis? The

carnival mirror of my imagination produces distorted glimpses of Billy/not Billy. Billy/not Billy.

I was allowed to see Thomas a couple of times a month, but only on days decided by Lizzie. And only ever at the house. There were certain ground rules now, all of them mandated by her: I was never to mention Conor; I was never to bring him with me; I was never to say anything about how I lived my life.

Thomas and I spent our visits digging out a vegetable patch a few metres square. We were going to grow giant vegetables, bean stalks, giants even. *Fee Fi Fo Fum*. Conor and I had bought the brightly coloured seed packets at the garden centre in Walthamstow one rainy Saturday afternoon.

I helped Thomas make shallow seed drills about the length of a fingernail and we planted carrot seeds. We covered the drills with a thin layer of soil and I filled up his small watering can with water. Thomas took the can from me carefully, gripping the handle tightly so as not to spill a drop. He sprinkled the earth with water and stopped every so often to stare at the ground as if expecting green shoots to appear spontaneously. Stepping intently along the line of seeds in his blue dungarees, he was a study of innocent loveliness and I felt an immense desire to protect him, this gentle and introspective child-man.

We filled some small pots with seed compost and put four pumpkin seeds in each, spacing them well apart. Then we did the same with our courgette seeds. Last of all, we sowed some rows of rocket, each row about a metre long. Thomas placed each seed with meticulous care, as if his life depended on it.

'Will there be green shoots tomorrow or the next day?' he asked, grinning up at me, hugging my waist.

'You need to be patient, chicken. It'll take a little longer than that.'

'Oh.'

'You need to water them when I'm not here.'

'I won't forget. Steve can help me.'

I felt a sharp little punch to the solar plexus: Steve was Lizzie's new boyfriend; an estate agent with designer stubble and hair gelled up like a corn husk. He was eight years her junior and I had no doubt Lizzie had told him all the gory details of our breakup. He was flinty and guarded around me, like I was going to pounce on him the moment he turned his back. It was clear he didn't like me and the feeling was mutual. I wasn't convinced Steve would help Thomas water the seeds, and if our little gardening project failed I'd be the bringer of false promises, the bringer of disappointment.

Thomas didn't really ask me much about the rest of my life; he was too young. The official line was that mummy and daddy had just grown apart, that I lived alone and was working as an educational consultant. The last part, at least, was true although Thomas didn't really know what it meant.

I let Lizzie create her little falsehoods. I didn't have much choice. The truth wasn't possible. The truth would separate me from my son; my father-in-law would see to that. All I wanted was the chance to be with Thomas, to spend a few hours being his father again. I found it very difficult to adjust to living apart. Every time I saw him, something else had changed: a little spurt in his height, a new maturity in his face, or a new interest in something at school. I was the one who always lagged behind, always had to play catch-up.

He was good at drawing, sketching out his own comic strips with his favourite superheroes. Now he had a more serious interest in art. His school reports talked about his love of painting, papier mâché, working with clay. I wondered if he might one day be an artist or a designer. I could to take him up to London, to the National Gallery or the Tate, to look at some of the great artists. But that didn't fit with the rules.

And at the tube station, at Berwick Street market, at the Odeon Leicester Square, the carnival mirror of my imagination produces distorted glimpses of Billy/no, not Billy. Billy/no, not...

A breeze stirred the broom and its little clusters of yellow, vanilla-scented flowers. I liked being outside with Thomas. It allowed us space away from Steve and Lizzie. When they were there, I invariably felt unwelcome like an interloper in the place I used to call home. They were always watching the clock, keen for me to go.

'Daddy!' Thomas had found a ladybird on the tip of his forefinger and watched it with solemn reverence as it crawled over his palm. Then, suddenly, its black and red wing cases swung open to reveal the hind wings and body underneath. Its wings beat to a blur and it was gone, darting through the air and away across the lawn. Beautiful creature.

It was almost time to go. Thomas and I went into the kitchen. Claia Bourne was the cheerless graveyard of our marriage. I poured Thomas a glass of orange juice and put a couple of biscuits on a plate. Steve came in, half-glancing at me before turning his attention to Thomas. 'Hey, Tommy, how's it going, mate?'

'Good.' Thomas's voice was very quiet. Like all children, he picked up on any difficulty between grown-ups so I tried to keep things light. I didn't want Thomas to think the awkwardness was because of him. I knew how the children of failed marriages could be; I'd taught enough of them.

'We've planted all our seeds,' I said. 'Thomas was hoping you could help him with the watering schedule.'

Steve blanked me and winked at Thomas, pinching him on the cheek. 'Sure I will, son.'

He's not your son. Don't call him 'son'.

Lizzie made her entrance: low-cut black vest and figure-hugging grey jeans; Doc Martens; a silver ankh dangling over her cleavage. I'd seen it all before with parents at school - Lizzie was wearing the uniform of the thirty-something divorcee trying to recapture her lost youth, and keep up with her young lover.

'Are you off now, then?' She'd been waiting all afternoon to get rid of me. I knelt down and gave Thomas a big hug.

'Remember to water the seeds like I told you.'

'When are you coming back to help, daddy?' He seemed suddenly so unsure. I looked up at Lizzie, waiting for a signal. She looked harried as if Thomas and I had been plotting against her. Her eyes met Steve's briefly before he slipped silently from the room.

'Daddy will be back soon,' she said, keeping her voice

211

as light as possible.

'But when?'

'Soon.'

'When's soon?'

'Thomas that's enough! Daddy's a very busy man.' I looked away from her. She was making it sound like I didn't have time for him. The person who didn't have time for him was Steve. Perhaps he resented competing for Lizzie's affections. Perhaps he wanted children of his own instead of minding the child of another man - a queer, a poofter, a faggot. I used to picture the day she'd announce she was marrying him; the dreaded moment.

'Don't worry,' I said. 'I'll be back very soon and Steve will help you with the watering, like he promised.' I made sure Lizzie heard. Thomas came outside and I hugged him one more time before Lizzie sent him back into the house. She looked at me, and I really didn't know her any more.

'When can I see him next?' I said.

'I'll have a look at the diary and let you know.'

'You know, it would be better for him if there was a more regular arrangement.'

It doesn't hurt to try.

'I'll let you know, Jack.'

ii

I don't notice it at first; something stuck to the windscreen. The wipers won't shift it. Screenwash doesn't help. I get out to take a closer look and it's a delightful little obscenity, almost certainly a message for me; a used condom.

212

The carnival mirror of my imagination...

I look around the car, under the car, all along the length of The Avenue skirting the golf course.

That old goat of a golf course.

Billy stops suddenly and lies down on his back. The chirping of grasshoppers fills the air and the bright little chirp-chirp, chirp-chirp rhythm is lazy and hot and hypnotic. 'Fuck me,' Billy whispers. 'Fuck me right here. Right now.'

And there's the white-blond hair, and the wiry frame marching up The Avenue, turning into the bushes, and I run after him. My boots stick in the mud. There's mud on my jeans. He's just ahead of me, moving in that otherworldly way, and I grab him by the arm and turn him roughly.

And someone I've never seen before says, 'Jesus Christ, what's your problem, mate?'

iii

Comptons opened a couple of years ago on the site of the old Swiss Tavern. Even before it became a fully-fledged gay pub, it was always known in Soho as 'not entirely straight'. Jack finds Conor in the bar upstairs.

'It's in a 1960s block, nice and roomy,' Jack is telling him, taking a swig from his bottle of Molson, 'and it's still got 120-odd years left on the lease.'

'Is this Walbrook?'

'Yeah. It's great. Floor to ceiling windows in the

213

bedroom and the sitting room is huge, with a balcony.'

'Sounds fantastic. How much?'

'Sixty thousand.'

'Wow. Big bucks.'

'I've arranged for us both to go and look at it on Saturday.'

iv

I never went back to Roughton Road after that last phone call with Sandie. I resigned the following week and she did a deal with the local authority to parachute in a new deputy.

I worked as a supply teacher for a while to tide me over until I got set up to start work as a private education consultant. For months now, Conor and I had been renting a tiny one-bedroom flat in Snaresbrook.

v

I was unaccountably nervous in Ronald Flint's office ('Mr Skinflint' behind his back to long-suffering Midland Bank customers and staff.) He put me in mind of a reptile clinging to a sunny rock: impassive but ready to dart - tongue and/or jaw extended - whenever his prey came within reach. Rumour had it, he was having an affair with his secretary Jennifer Jones, faded Tippi Hedren to his portly Rod Taylor.

Over the years, my encounters with Ronald Flint had been cordial enough: he was the one who approved my mortgage on Claia Bourne. But now I was no longer the successful deputy head with a steady income. I was a self-employed hopeful striking out on my own. I wore a sober tie and a dark blue shirt which hid the beads of perspiration running down my sides.

I worried for nothing.

I told him how much I expected to earn as a consultant and he shook my hand so hard it made my arm hurt. 'Of course we can green light a second mortgage for you, Mr Huntley. I'll have the paperwork ready for you next week.'

I told him I was living alone, naturally. I was still a stranger in my own life. *Stranger in a strange land.* It was always best to omit Conor in my dealings with the outside world - if I wanted to be accepted. Conor had to remain my careful, thoughtful secret.

I almost cartwheeled down George Lane. I picked up a bottle of Beaujolais and an Indian takeaway. We were going to have our own home!

'I'm sure it's going to be wonderful.' Conor chinked his beer bottle against mine and looked at me with his soft brown eyes. And in that moment - here it comes - I knew without any question that I loved him.

Perhaps the Furies are never that far away. Perhaps 'endless anger', 'jealous rage', and 'vengeful destruction' watch and wait for all men. And perhaps sometimes they are met and matched by that softest but fiercest of complicities - when love is answered by love.

We ate our takeaway and drank our Beaujolais and laughed and made love.

I felt exhilarated - a little uncomfortable too - but exhilarated to be living with another man, shopping together, going to the pictures together, dining at a table for two together: it was all so new, so wonderfully new, but also awkward-feeling like a pair of shoes that need breaking in. Conor had a simple inner certainty about who he was. And I took my courage from that. I was becoming a better man because of Conor. (I was becoming a man because of Conor.) Meanwhile the newspapers were full of appalling stories - police arresting men for holding hands in public; MPs talking about re-criminalising gay sex; straw polls in the press claiming two-thirds of the public despised homosexuals. In the midst of the public loathing and exaggerated moral outrage, Conor was my hope of a happier future.

vi

Conor leans forward and rests his beer on the table. 'I saw Billy today,' he says bluntly. His words fall like a bucket of cold water.

'When?'

'He's back at college. I saw him going into one of the seminar rooms. He didn't see me.'

'Stay well away.'

'We're not on the same course or even in the same year. I'm hardly ever there. Just going in for tutorials on my dissertation.'

'My only priority is to keep you safe.'

Billy.

But Jack can't let the thought go. Jack can't see any easy way out. 'Why don't we go on holiday for a couple of weeks?' he says. A first strategy. A stopgap.

Conor is doubtful. 'I'm not sure. I've got tons to do on my dissertation.'

'You can take some time off, surely. I know just the place. Bring some books. You can study while we're there.'

The sky is a clear, emphatic blue, even this early in the day.

chapter sixteen

i

My lesson with Hakesh was tougher than usual: relentless backhand and forehand drills followed by a series of aggressive practice games. He always liked to push me to my limits. 'If you'd started training as a kid, you could have turned pro.' Then he'd rib me: 'Too bad you're past it!'

I was glad to hit the showers. I turned the lever and felt the powerful jets easing and kneading my upper back.

Conor and I were going to Norfolk - *very flat, Norfolk* - our first holiday together, and it would get him as far away as possible from Billy Soanes, for the time being at least - go any further and your feet are in the sea.

I was looking forward to showing him some of my favourite places: the Highcliff Pavilion, Cromer's Victorian pier, the village of Salthouse and the wild sand and shingle of Blakeney Point.

I hadn't seen Nigel since Billy, the martyr of Santiago, crashed the anniversary party. He was almost certainly avoiding me, coming to the club when he knew I was least likely to be there.

But this time his luck had run out. He glanced at me and nodded, not realising who I was; I hadn't bothered to shave one lazy weekend and Conor said he liked it, so I'd grown a beard.

When recognition finally dawned, he moved his towel instinctively to cover his genitals, even though we'd seen each other naked in the showers a thousand times before.

'Hi Nigel,' I said, as casually as I could.

'Oh, hi.' He was a red-faced choirboy, caught with his trousers down. 'I didn't recognise you… with the erm… facial hair.'

'Are you here for a lesson?' I asked.

'Finished a doubles match,' he said. 'Just a friendly, you know, couple of sets.' Then he turned to go.

'Aren't you going to shower?'

'No… I don't think I've got time. In a bit of a rush.'

I dried myself, watching Nigel a few lockers away, body half-turned to the wall, pulling on his y-fronts and trousers.

'How's work?' I said.

'Same old, same old… you know.'

He was looking down, concentrating on his socks, shuffling his feet purposefully into his slip-ons.

'How's Sandie?'

'She's fine.'

He buttoned up his shirt.

'And the kids?'

'All fine.'

He picked up his rucksack and glanced over his shoulder. 'Bye then.'

I wasn't surprised. He'd always had enough 'poofter' jokes and 'limp-wrist' put-downs to sink the Bismarck. But it still hurt. We had been friends. And now it counted for nothing - after all those years. I hadn't realised it was contingent on my playing by certain rules, playing the game his way.

'I'm sorry if I make you uncomfortable,' I called to him. But I wasn't sorry; I wanted him to know he was acting like a jerk. He stopped abruptly and turned round to face me.

'Why did you do it, Jack?' he said. 'Why did you lie to everyone? To your wife, your friends, to me? I thought we were mates. Why did you lie to me?'

'What if I'd told you the truth? Would it have made a difference?' He heaved a sigh, shaking his head as if to shake me off for good. 'Well?' I said, pushing the point. 'Well, Nigel? Would it?'

The door to the changing room banged shut behind him. I threw my towel across the room and slammed the base of my fist into the locker door. This was the world I lived in now. Awkwardnesses. Silences. Being the 'other', the freak.

(Conor and I had driven out to a restaurant in Chingford, only to be told it was a family venue and they didn't have a table for 'two men together'.)

I sat down on the bench and stared at the wall. To hell with Nigel. To hell with Lizzie. To hell with all of them.

I retrieved my towel and got dressed. It was time to go and collect my boyfriend. The idea of 'having a boyfriend' would take some getting used to but I liked the way it sounded.

ii

Conor waves at Jack as he walks across the car park of the polytechnic. The day is hot for the time of year, and white clouds bubble up jubilantly over the city. Jack has booked Pear Tree Cottage again - as a kind of delicious revenge: if Lizzie had Claia Bourne and had installed Steve there, Jack would take Conor to the one-time love nest in Norfolk.

'My tutor's off sick today,' Conor says as he climbs into the passenger seat of the BMW. 'His secretary says he'll be back tomorrow so I left the dissertation on his desk and the address of the cottage. He can post it back to me with his comments. I'll work on the revisions when we're not swimming in the sea or having a nice long lunch.'

'Or making love.' Jack sighs, resting his hand on Conor's thigh. Conor laughs.

'You're an old-fashioned romantic!'

Jack wants to kiss him but someone might see and old habits die hard. Conor fishes two Mars bars and a couple of sorry-looking cheese sandwiches out of his rucksack. 'For the journey - North East London Polytechnic's finest,' he says triumphantly.

The mid-afternoon traffic is unusually light as they follow the North Circular onto the M11. The suburbs of Loughton and Epping quickly give way to sunny countryside. A gentle breeze makes the wheat ripple like a golden wave far out at sea. Small hamlets and solitary farms punctuate the landscape, far apart and beneath a sky of the most intense cornflower blue. Cruising at sixty along the motorway, it feels like they are leaving all their troubles behind. On days like this, leaving London felt like a release. The vast airlessness of the city; that terrible heat trap. It was good to be heading towards the coast where the sea air was cooler and the nights were quieter.

They stop briefly to pick up some groceries in Cromer and finally pull up outside the cottage just after five.

'Wow,' says Conor. 'You weren't joking when you said it was on the cliffs.'
'It's perfectly safe. And the views are lovely.'
Jack was always amazed by the difference in temperature at the coast. The early evening is heavy with damp. The dusk is turning liquid and they grab their jackets, buttoning them up against the sharpening breeze as they walk out to the church.

iii

Jack lights the fire when they get back and there's soon a good blaze in the grate to take the chill off the room. They sit together in silence, drinking wine, watching the tall flames jostle and dance as the small, dry logs pop and spit. Jack tops up their glasses and they go into the wonky little kitchen to cook supper. They fry onions, garlic, peppers and minced beef for a good old spaghetti bolognese and listen to the Mark Goodier show on Radio

One, and eat too much, and drink too much and it's blissful and they climb into the creaky double bed just after midnight and Jack embraces Conor, and feels that reassuring warmth of his body by his side.

iv

Light slices through a chink in the curtains. The sea has mounted up against the beach, sticking its neck out you could say, a reckless spring tide washing blue over gold.

Conor is still asleep, his chest rising and falling in a gentle hee-haw rhythm, the covers thrown off his slim, naked body because it has turned unseasonally warm.

Jack kisses him and he opens his eyes sleepily in answer, unsure for a moment where he is. His sleepy confusion makes him seem helpless and hopelessly desirable. Jack wants to take care of him, to love him, to defend him from all perils and dangers of this night.

He kisses him again. Conor finds Jack's hardness and grips him gently. Jack puts his hand on the back of the boy's head and guides him down gently until he feels the moist warmth of Conor's mouth surrounding his shaft.

Jack pulls out just before the moment of reckoning and his milky saltiness spatters Conor's chin.

Conor comes quickly in reply and they go to the shower, exploring each other still with tender fingers and tongues under the hot water.

v

They dry each other with thick fluffy towels. Conor works slowly and methodically, Jack's thoughtful boy.

Conor is so very careful and that amount of thought and care changes things, amounts to something else. And this is not lost on Jack.

Jack puts on his jeans and a clean tee shirt and watches Conor dressing slowly: his silken briefs sliding up his legs and stretching across his butt; his faded, used-look Levis outlining the contours of his thighs, his green polo shirt snug against his chest.

Jack plans to take Conor up to Roman Camp, to his favourite bench looking out over the densely wooded hillside and down to the great openness of the North Sea in flood. He steps out onto the balcony and the sky is clear, emphatically blue, even this early in the day. It is a good day for a long, meandering walk.

Beyond the little cottage garden, the tide has reached its full height, brimming and glittering in the morning sun, and then he sees it: the fabric of the soft-top slashed - the car, like his hope, in tatters - the slim scimitar of the knife stabbing the garden table and something's pinned under the blade: Conor's likeness, what else?

Billy.

Billy's message is unmistakable. For a brief instant, Jack doesn't know what to do. He swallows and tastes fear at the back of his throat. Then he wonders, Is this it? He had thought this was the beginning of happiness, but what if it is the end? Is this really how it all ends, love, sex, hope, happiness, the future?

Jack will die to save Conor from Billy and his Furies.

For a while now, it's been on the cards, dear reader, that these terrors of Billy's will be met by love.

But here, now, is a 'turn up for the books' as you might say. For the first time in his life, Jack is the vessel of 'the real thing'. Jack loves Conor, not as he loved Lizzie (because it was easy?), not as he desired Billy - *'Fuck me,' Billy whispers. 'Fuck me right here. Right now.'* - but as an honest man, a self-respecting, honourable and truthful man.

'Trouble,' he says.

Conor's smile collapses as he sees the look on Jack's face.

'*Billy*,' Jack says. And throws Conor the car keys and says, 'Whatever happens, get out of here. Get help.'

'I'm not leaving without you.'

'Please, just do as I tell you.'

Jack grips Conor's hand and feels the lovely warmth of it, the lovely, redeeming warmth of his thoughtful boy.

He opens the bedroom door ajar. The landing is empty. And then he feels the adrenaline racing hotly to his heart and his addicted heart responding, and he half-expects to see Billy just there but instead there are only bright motes of dust, jubilant in the sunlit air. And why are they 'jubilant'? you might ask.

The floorboards creak under foot and Jack holds his breath, and then he hears the curious tap-tap-tapping drifting up from the floor below.

Tap - tap - tap.

Faintly at first.

Tap - tap - tap.

More insistent now.

Tap - tap - tap.

They see the front door is wide open, shaken by the wind from the sea, which is pushing, pushing the tide water up, up and over the warm sand. Bluest water in bluest light. Up, up, further up and over gold, high enough now to overwhelm the sea defences themselves.

Tap - tap - tap.

So here is their escape. Here is where Jack spirits Conor out of harm's way. But the door seems suddenly very far off and these are only mortal boys, not gods. Everything seems drawn out; at an immense distance. It is as if millions of years have passed since Jack first saw Billy. Einstein is chuckling, 'It's all relative!'

He is the blondest boy the man has ever seen. He looks at the man with peculiar eyes. It is as if he is looking into the world from somewhere unimaginable.

Tap - tap - tap.
Tap - tap - tap.

Jack steps with infinite caution towards the open door.

Tap - tap - tap.

Conor is so close behind him, Jack can feel his warmth.

Tap - tap - tap.

Something moves so quickly in front of Jack, it's unfeasible and unholy, and it's Billy of course; Billy

227

bringing down the poker onto Jack's skull and the world explodes in showers of light and Jack falls to his knees, his hand rising instinctively to the point of impact but there is no pain, only a feeling of astonishment as he feels the warm wetness of his own blood on his fingers, and he looks up in time to see the poker falling again and he is floating, falling, floating and he doesn't know which way is up and which way is down, and what is real and what is a dream, what is warm-blooded boy and what is wraith, and his face is numb against the cold of the stone floor, and these stones have an odd sponginess to them, and he struggles to move the inflating balloon of his head, and he sees Billy and Conor dancing like lovers, and Billy's eyes are full of love or fury - Virgil's 'endless anger', 'jealous rage', 'vengeful destruction' come to the temporal world to destroy Conor, Jack's thoughtful boy with *something akin to love in the care he takes.*

Apart from Thomas, Conor is the only creature Jack has ever loved with a whole and true heart.

Why is Conor dancing with Billy? Why is Billy clothed in purple and scarlet; adorned with gold and jewels and pearls, holding in his hand a golden cup full of abominations and the impurities of his prostitution?

And why is Conor clutching his throat and struggling to breathe? If only to breathe.

B-r-e-a-t-h-e.

Sense returns for a moment to the addled sponge bleeding inside Jack's skull, and he hauls himself to his feet and here he is, at last, dear reader.

Now, at last, we see him in his truth. He was only ever tenuously Jack Huntley, you see.

He is the Great Colossus Love.
Beloved of mother earth.
And somewhere in the streets children are singing.

Billy has caught Conor's ankle and brought him low. Billy raises the white blade of his knife. Conor lifts his arms to defend himself. Billy raises the knife high, high above his head, high, gripping it in both hands, high in readiness, high, and Jack hears the word, 'No!' And for a moment he doesn't recognise the sound at all and then, for the first time in his life, he recognises the sound of his own voice.

'No.'

Jack strikes the knife from Billy's hand. There is no pain now. He strides outside, in pursuit of Billy and Conor, and Billy is wrapping a coloured cord around Conor's neck and the mounting pressure in Jack's cranium increases his acuity so that he sees everything as if he is divine. He has a deity's sight: Conor is flailing blindly, Billy is strangling him. And the Great Colossus Love casts Billy easily aside so that he reels and stumbles and falls.

Conor is wrapped in the great limbs of the Colossus now, cradled as if he were a child and here, illuminated absolutely, is the sublime mystery of love.

'I loved you, Jack. Why couldn't you love me too?' The voice is Billy's, who else?

Billy watches Jack holding Conor and his face is

reconfigured as sorrow, bewilderment, all unmet desire. He looks at his own hands almost tenderly, then he comes for Jack, knife bright in his grasp, and Billy and Jack are together again, like lovers, one last time, and the blade slides and the blood is cherry stones falling, and blossom on the wind and the sea brimming, blue over gold, and the defences are breached; breath to breath; lovers in the intimacy of despair; and Billy is reconfigured again as frightened child, lonely child, and there is only one way this story can end; and Billy knows it too. The Colossus surrenders at last to the pale wraith, the blondest boy the man has ever seen and, in surrendering, the Great Colossus saves his thoughtful and beautiful and lovely boy, Conor.

Think on this. Innocence has departed. For all his fucking and taking, Jack never really gave away anything of himself. He was always the fucking and fighting ingénu. The Great Beginner.

But all that was Jack is dissolved in love. And now Jack and Billy must tumble over the cliff edge. Why set the end of the story on a cliff if no one is going over the edge?

Jack and Billy must fall. The Fall is long and slow. In the film of the book, the actors and a montage of images would punctuate, and extend, The Fall. (The images would be accompanied by discordant music, from Kabuki theatre perhaps; *Farewell My Concubine*.)

The sea.

The great blue basin of the sea.

The immateriality of the sky.

No horizon line between sea and sky, no demarcation between water and air, the physical and the immaterial.

A bright light.

A great silence. Like a vow.

Die Große Stille.

Billy's face, a white oval.

Pale as pearl.

Billy's hair, white fire.

Jack.

A handsome man.

Nothing more, nothing less.

The irresistible religious overtones of The Fall.

Fall and resurrection.

The Fall.

A singular pair of feathers turning.

Farther and farther. Father and father.

They Fall.

They have fallen.

A great big 'fuck you' to life, the universe and everything.

vi

Conor looks over the cliff edge.

He looks down at the broken body of poor Billy and at the broken body of his lovely, lovely Jack.

Jack.

And he begins to cry.

And the world is full of weeping.

FIN

Coming 2025

Who's Afraid of Shirley Jackson?

A Novel by

William Jackson

Cambridge Queer Press

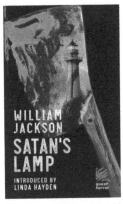

A lonely rock lighthouse is said to be haunted by Cornish locals. That's why they call it 'Satan's Lamp'.

In a small rural community, a schoolboy is at war with his own body. What will it take to fulfil his misbegotten destiny?

The 1589 text translated into modern English provides the first feminist insight into love between the sexes.

A biographical exploration of the spiritual woman behind the legendary Swedish film actor.

Image credits:

Page 16: Cottonbro Studio
https://www.pexels.com/photo/5044960

Page 32: Anna Nekrashevich
https://www.pexels.com/photo/8058913

Page 46: Анастасия Климец
https://www.pexels.com/photo/14118017

Page 60: Ave Calvar Martinez
https://www.pexels.com/photo/3497624

Page 78: Cottonbro studio
https://www.pexels.com/photo/3692751

Page 88: Daria Liudnaya
https://www.pexels.com/photo/8187678

Page 102: Melike Benli
https://www.pexels.com/photo/10079195

Page 116: Ricardo Ribeiro
https://www.pexels.com/photo/5258907

Page 126: Eva Bronzini
https://www.pexels.com/photo/6914957

Page 136: Atrina Me
https://www.pexels.com/photo/15476191

Page 146: Mad Knoxx
https://www.pexels.com/photo/18031604

Page 174: Anna Alexes
https://www.pexels.com/photo/8080278

Page 190: Emma Bauso
https://www.pexels.com/photo/2253850

Page 202: Sebastian Arie Voortman
https://www.pexels.com/photo/715546

Page 216: Pixabay
https://www.pexels.com/photo/274127